The awakening of century old curse...

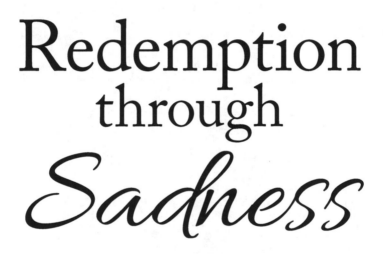

Redemption
through
Sadness

Melanie Sacay Lizardo

author**HOUSE**®

AuthorHouse™
1663 Liberty Drive
Bloomington, IN 47403
www.authorhouse.com
Phone: 833-262-8899

This is a work of fiction. All of the characters, names, incidents, organizations, and dialogue in this novel are either the products of the author's imagination or are used fictitiously.

Published by AuthorHouse 02/19/2021

ISBN: 978-1-6655-1773-7 (sc)
ISBN: 978-1-6655-1772-0 (e)

Library of Congress Control Number: 2021903556

Print information available on the last page.

Any people depicted in stock imagery provided by Getty Images are models, and such images are being used for illustrative purposes only. Certain stock imagery © Getty Images.

This book is printed on acid-free paper.

For Mamala and Papalo

Contents

Prologue

Ashley Parker-Dmitri, an interior designer of the prestigious NYC Company, got a strange deal from a billionaire that is residing in New Zealand. Even with her refusal, the company insist to send her to the said country.

Arriving in Auckland **Airport,** a driver and a butler picked her up, which added to her frustration about the said project. Who would have thought that she is in this foreign country without even the name and personal information to whom she is going to work with? With all the work she handled, a profile and data sheet where given which enable her to see the interest of the client. Studying her client, being prepared for the concept of design is an ace for her but this set-up seems to be a shot gun and strange.

It is a mixed of emotion. She is confused and curious. What is with this person that the CEO of the company trust him so well that sends employee to stay for 30 days with notable tour packages every weekend?

Acknowledgment

Be it known that writing a book is always a fascination of most Literature and Language Major. So, it is the same whisper that the author follows for the creation of this book. The author wish to extend her appreciation to:

- Lizardo and Sacay family, as the safe haven of rare minds for endless passion, deserves a recognition for nurturing the ambition of the writer;

- Author Solutions Philippines Inc., as the backbone of the project, justifies praise for a gamble on a dream that was not attested but fully trusted;

- Few but special friends (Joyce Noreen Ferolino, Sarah Embalzado) whom contributed on the personal growth of the author earn a celebration as this book will be a seal of camaraderie;

- Hande Deryagil, the person who gave all the support on the journey of the author, merits the limitless words of gratefulness.

Chapter One

"Sometimes we neglect the blessing in unpredicted events. We see it eccentric and name it as a disaster without us knowing it will direct us to ultimate joy."

Strange Day

"With the certainty of the calendar, there lies the uncertainty of tomorrow."

"DRIIIIIIIIIIN!" ASHLEY WOKE UP WITH the loud noise of her digital clock. Hitting its stop button, she forces herself to open her heavy eye to glance on the time- 6:30 in the morning.

"Another day of battling the unknown." She utters to herself.

After some while looking at the lone curtained window of her two-bedroom apartment, she got up. With her height of five feet eight, this gave her an advantage on the view of her humble suite. Examining the weather, (it is odd that it is gloomy) it's about to rain where in fact she checks the weather forecast last night, and says, "It's a clear and sunny day". Commonly the temperature runs around 21-27°C until mid-month of September. "We are still in the first week." Out of frustration, she walked heavily to her home satellite office.

"Well I guess running isn't a choice." She lurched along the empty aisle, which is mostly plain because of the minimalist design she adopted.

As she enters the other room, she easily spotted the abstract painting given to her by her University sponsor. It draws a smile on her face. It is the main reason she decided to make it a centerpiece of this room-to remind her of those hard times.

Her life is no luxury. She is an orphan at the age of fourteen due to a drastic accident that her parents got involved. Leaving her at the custody of her old maiden aunt from her mother side, she needs to work her ass out during college and earn a degree in Interior Design at Fashion Institute of Technology. She is proud of what she has become.

Logging in to her personal computer, she checked her schedule for the day. "Great! I am going to have another project." With excitement, she opens her creative folders.

She tried to browse over her old business proposals to get some ideas that for her meeting with the new client. She needs to impress the director because according to the rumors this is a family member. This person is dear to the director.

"Let me try to get some information from Vicky." Picking up her mobile phone.

Vicky is her assistant for three years. This woman holds every information about the office. She is a trusted friend even with her tactless mouth. "Hey, Vic! So tell me about this client that I am going to meet."

"Ash, I am about to call you to ask the same thing. People from the office thought you have the profile." Vicky utters.

"Interesting. Never got anything on my hand. Better meet them later then" she said with a little curiosity. "Vicky, be in by ten. Do not be late this time. Bring folder fourteen and twenty." Her final remark.

"Ash, before you go. Meeting will be at the penthouse." Vicky bidding goodbye.

"Alright." Therefore, the rumors might be true. This client and the CEO are related. The penthouse is at the 17th floor of the building her company owns and the home of the company owner. Not that they all occupy the entire building but the management able to have the 1st to 11th floor rented by other businesses.

She got up and decided to make some breakfast. She strides over her kitchen and prepare her rice cooker. Her close friend started to love eating Asian Rice because of her. Her food speaks for her culture- Filipino-American.

As she washes her rice and get it set-up for the machine, she remembers her mother.

A perfect tanned 5'3 individual that is full of positivity and values. She is her life model. Her late mom has not scold or shout at her. Instead, she whispers words of love and affection. She wished to have her more especially now that she needs someone for advices and for answers.

Her dad is a bubbly person from Tennessee. Common compatriot with the love for travelling. The reason he met her mom in one of his missionary works in the Philippines. She never got the chance to visit the land of her mother or any other country due to finances. All she got is a picture of her mom in her hometown called-Siargao.

After the preparation of her heavy meal, she set her Granite Countertops where she lays her food over in the middle her self-designed kitchen island with white and black motif. She was able to prepare beef broccoli, pineapple slices, and two cups of rice. Not a normal American diet, but thankful for her Asian blood that does not give her any gain.

Ashley is now on her way to the office. Taking her matte black Jaguar F-type, she drives out the basement of the apartment building. The moment the car hits the road the heavy rain pours out. "This is a strange day!"

Unknown

"Fear of the unknown starts with knowing."

Arriving in the office at the right time smoothly is a blessing even with the heavy rain in NYC. People in the building started coming in even if it is still early. Ashley is impress by this. "What is with today?" She finally reached her own office.

As one of the Senior Designer of the company with the rate of 90,000 USD per project, she managed to grow her assets and stock in the market. People wonder why her home is underrated. One thing- she do not need huge place without someone sharing it. It suffocates her looking at an empty place. At the age of twenty-eight, she never had a romantic relationship. Not that she is unattractive, in fact, she is above average, and she just never felt something special with anyone. She fancy boys but never felt spark with them. Maybe she values talk more than looks. People often name her as asexual and sapiosexual. She does not care to study those identities. All she knows she will commit when she felt something special with someone.

After some while, her assistant got in to her office, which stopped her from thinking what is out in the open.

"Ash, good morning! I got the folders prepared and I am not late, ey?" Vicky draws near to reach her table and set the folder in the table.

Ashley took at her watch and state, "Two minutes late. Not bad. Are you ready?" She looks at Vicky in the eye.

"Yes, I am excited to meet this Mysterious Prince that can be my future husband." Vicky swaying her hips seductively as she picks up the folders needed for the meeting.

Ashley smirk as she sees the motivation on her friend. She told herself inside, "I wonder why this woman is still single well in fact she looks like a Victoria Secret Model."

"Let's!" Ashley cheers as she stand-up from her office chair.

The two walk along the hallway to reach the elevator going to the penthouse. As the door of the elevator closed, she felt weird sensation that she never felt before. Is she nervous? Is she scared of what is what to come?

Reaching the access door to the penthouse made her shivers. It is the second time that she was able to talk to the CEO- Jonas Hartman. The first was when she owns her position as the Senior Designer of the company on her 1st year anniversary. This is a goal-setter because most of the people awarded with the positions are well-known tenure designers who have stayed in the company for over a decade. She always calls it as luck.

"Should I open the door now?" Vicky startled her with the note.

"Right. Open it." She is beyond surprise that this woman is not feeling any hesitation on this act.

They walk inside the greenhouse-inspired penthouse. This is decorated and detailed by various tensile strengths tempered glass, high ceilings, an undulating ceiling and potted plants. This is a well-celebrated design of her company but not something that she would like to own for herself.

It does not bother her criticizing the design knowing that it was her profession. There are a lot more that she can do with this house given the chance. It would give it a break of green if they would install a corner of safari motif or even a dull yellow. Green when it is too much being overwhelming.

They reached the bar area of the CEO where he is staying most of his time. She even wonders if the CEO have alcohol control problem.

"Ashley, Mi amor! Sit down." The Cuban accent of the CEO revealed.

She roams her eye around looking for the client. "Joe, where is the client?" She said as she takes a sit beside him.

"Focused to the business too much? That is what I like about you. But dear, have a drink first and let me call the client." The husky voice of the Young CEO enters her ear.

"Joe, I don't drink at work. I still have a long day to go." She is firm on her stand and principles. She ventures her sight to the Joe and saw him checking her secretary out.

"Who is this lady you got in here?" Flirtatious call of the owner to the secretary.

"Victoria Dankworth. It is a pleasure to meet you, sir. I am Ashley's Secretary for over 3 years now." Reaching her hand over to the mister.

"The pleasure is mine. I do think about the first name bases that you have with Ashley." A serious note that made the secretary a little shocked.

"Joe, don't scare her please. Besides you how I do my work. I do not give a fuck with salutation. I don't even give it to you." She explained.

"I am trying to be humorous but I think can never be. My apologies, Victoria." He smiles while he touches the back of his neck.

"Let me call the client then. Please make yourself comfortable." The young businessperson stands and pull his phone up.

"Ash, does it mean that the client isn't here?" Vicky starts on asking. It means there is more. "I find this unprofessional. Why there is no proper meeting like what is indicated on our rules."

Her secretary is right. According to the client agreement, they need to be present on the first meeting. For the designer to prepare their proposals, personal data sheet, architectural folder, preferences will be giver prior to the contract signing. It did not happen.

The moment she is about to answer- Jonas is done and remarked, "Great. Ashley, here is your ticket, weekend allowance, buffer fund, contract and the location."

"Hang on; you didn't give me the profile yet." She opens the folder containing her ticket and other documents. "What? New Zealand? Jonas, this is not right. You haven't discussed about this."

"I am your employer it means I still hold your schedule. One month in New Zealand, double rate, free accommodation and just one house." The final word of the CEO.

"It means I need to fly tomorrow in a place where I don't know who I am working with?" She started to scream.

"Yes, dear." She sharply looks at the man in the eye. "It is my cousin. I think that information is enough. Victoria will come along anyway so what is with the scare."

"Please excuse me I need a breather." She walks out of the penthouse bringing with anxieties and worry.

The Call

"Often we need harsh real advices rather than sweet flattery."

One of the benefits of being an interior designer, she can easily go home when it is not necessary to stay in the office. After the said conversation, she sends her secretary home for her to prepare. She might not like the concept of how this project landed on her but somehow she knows it leaves her with no choice.

She is currently in her apartment and walking back and forth in front of her transparent sliding door closet, which has the unique oblique edges.

"What are you scared of Ash?" She is having an internal battle. "You dreamt of travelling across the globe and here it is."

Struggling about this travel sound silly for someone in her position. It is normal to travel for work. Especially that her company is internationally marketed. Only few people know about the anxieties. More like this becomes her phobia. No one cared to ask why she is scared to take a plane crossing the large ocean. It made it easy for her to hide about her past because of the distance she had established for the people at work.

The concept of travelling bothers her because of her lost. Her parents died in the ADC Airlines Flight 53 plane crash.

Her parents plan a charity work in Nigeria when the unforeseen event happened. Her mom being an English Professor and her dad as a missionary, they visit and travel together to reach more people that needs help.

It was then she realizes that her parent was not able to come home for two months that she started asking to her aunt.

That was the time where she realized that she no longer have both her parents. Even the months stole her awareness on the death of her parents, the grief when the newsbreak was unmeasurable.

She was startled when she heard her phone rings. "Hello." She answered without looking at the caller id.

"'Iha, I saw your message. Is there something wrong?" the voice of her aunt Lisa succored her.

"Aunty, I am troubled as to whether I should take the flight to New Zealand for a project. I am beyond scared to cross the big oceans."

"Don't you think it is about time to let go of the past? Just try it. Sleep throughout the flight." Flushed answer from her aunt. Which is what she likes about this woman. No filters, no sweet words just direct answer.

"Right! Can I meet you when I am back in the state?"

"I'll be happy to see you. Hoping you are not alone this time around." Here you go. The pressure is up with the pairing.

"That I can't promise."

"Iha, open your heart the way you open your eyes in design. Sooner you will settled when you have someone. When grave will demand my presence, I want you safe." The serious tone of the old maiden makes her shivers.

"Aunt Lee, what if I am destined to be like you?" she tried to convince her aunt about the blessing of being single.

"You don't know everything Ashley. You don't know." The conviction on the voice of the old maiden is completely gone and was exchange with deep sadness.

Her aunt's lifestyle always had her curious about her aunt's past. Even she lived with the woman, she is restricted to enter the room or talk about her past relationship. It is something that can trigger the emotion of the poor old woman. However, with all the years, this is something that she still pray for- "Someday she will receive a call that would open her up to the past of her Aunt Lee."

The Shadow

> *"It wasn't bad to search for what was beneath just make*
> *sure you know how to return to the surface."*

"Ash, the gates are now open. Are you still doubting whether we are going to board or not?" the voice of her impatient secretary echoed to her.

"I n-eed to take a break first. Let them get in then we can follow." Her lame excuse as she tried to hide her fear in the said flight.

After the said talk with her aunt, she prepared packing and tried to meditate on this action. This is a great development for her. Something that she needs to let go on the past and something that she need to pick up for the future. It will open more opportunity for her too. Knowing the company tried so many times on sending her on a project abroad, she always finds a way to decline the offer. A blessing for the junior designers in the company who is open for the said project. She always has names for recommendation.

"They are now calling for our names, Ash. What are we waiting for?" Irritated call of her friend. "Is there something I should know? What is wrong with you? I am concern." The nag of the tactless friend. "You are sweating so much Ashley."

Vicky, out of concern, wipe her sweat of the forehead and check her temperature in the same area. Then she responded, "No need for that. I think I am fine," she notes to her companion. Moreover, it gains a great stare of confusion.

"Let us cancel this trip if you felt bad about this plan. I will support you." This reminds her of the situation...

She saw a deep confusion and concern on the face of her companion. "Let us board now. We are here and I will not go backwards." She stands up and go straight the boarding gate.

"I am here. You need to tell me about what the heck is this." The gorgeous black American quoted to her with deep pool of emotion. "Not now, but soon after you feel like it." Added voice of the secretary. This is the main reason she is be-friended. Her heart and sensitivity.

Arriving in Auckland Airport, they are ushered by tall muscular driver that looks like a hired high security agent of the president of the United State. Okay, that might be an exaggeration but she felt that way. Speak for more for the butler, his name is- Rodrigo.

According to the handsome Caucasian guy, in his mid-30's, he will be the personal assistant that will take care of them all throughout the month.

"I don't actually think it would be necessary for us to have you Rodrigo. We can handle ourselves. We came here for work just like you are." Her irritated tone.

"As you said, I come here for work. It would be easier for us to just work together. Let me do mine and do yours." She was stunned by the answer of the butler. "Alright. Ms. Parker-Dmitri I would like to give you these papers." He continued.

"I guess this is the hotel reservation and house culprit?" she said while opening the folder with keys.

"That is the blueprint of the mansion. It will serve as your map on your rooms. You will be staying with the **Fernsby.**" The butler motion another set of keys. "This is for the Jaguar that they purchased for you to drive around. They made sure that it was the same brand as yours in the state."

This turn her face white. What is with this family that can afford to purchase a car just like hers? "I guess I don't have a say to this?"

"Just enjoy the generosity of the family." The final remark of the butler before the compartment window of the limo closed.

"Wow! Are we going to Buckingham?" the voice of the secretary is finally heard. On the other hand- maybe she was not paying attention.

"We are in New Zealand so obviously we aren't." she responded.

For a moment, she forgot about the nerve wrecking flight that she had. Seventeen hours' direct flight is not a joke but like what her auntie told her to just sleep it out and nerves will go away. It does work. Somehow, she enjoys the luxury of a first class flight with champagne.

She sighs and said, "It is all a shadow of the past."

Chapter Two

"Giving someone judgement even without knowing them dearly is a common thing to do. Most of the time, we fell miserable on building relationship with them."

Look at the Marks

*"Coincidence is a vague angle to look at especially
when there are too many leaving tracts."*

DUE TO THE LONG TRIP from NYC to New Zealand, Ashley was not aware that she dozes off. With around two hours, trip from the airport everything they see is pure astonishing greenery that is the last thing she remembers before she closed her eyes.

"Ash, we are here." As she felt a gentle shake from her arm. When she opens her eyes, she saw her secretary, which is sitting beside her on the limo. "I think you might want to use this." The woman gave her a mirror and her pouch of make-up.

Not that she is applying so much on her face, she just wanted to freshen up for the said meet and greet with the client. The client that made her feel angry and irritated.

"What is the time now in New Zealand?" when the secretary is about to answer the window of the driver roll down and Rodrigo answered instead.

"It is twelve noon. Exactly the time plotted in your schedule of arrival. I will escort you to your rooms. Our resident chef will visit you personally to ask for your food preference and food related information that we need to know. Same goes with bringing simple varieties of food for your lunch." Long statement of the man.

Rodrigo open the door to get out of the car. This confident person knows his work so well. She might not know fully how you can handle a butler. Nevertheless, sure she will have a great time with this person.

The next thing she knows Rodrigo is already offering her his hand for her to move out of the vehicle.

As she steps out of the car, she was welcomed by the huge semi-modern house, which is obviously renovated from a brick material. She can say that this huge house is here for hundred years.

The smell of the wood and leaves welcomes her nostrils. She can enjoy this. It is remarkable foreign aroma of warmth, earthy and reassuring base notes to perfumes, which are built on underlying notes of yelp, moss and wood oils. That are indispensable to perfumery include Sandalwood, Rosewood, Agarwood, Cane and Cedar.

"Welcome New Zealand!" she declares within herself as she takes a deep breath of the natural air.

They are now in the front of the old double door made of timber standing around 24-foot long. This look ancient but elegant with its gold plates around the frames. It instantly open, as they are 4 meters away of the entrance. "Fascinating."

"Not to interrupt you Ms. Parker-Dmitri, as you may glance to the right alley there parks the Car that looks identical to your car. You have the full papers inside under your name and the license from the bureau to give you rights on driving around." She gulps.

At the back of her mind, there are questions as to why this is necessary for her to have a driving license and a car under her name.

"In case you have request on the interior of the car and any modification, let me know and I'll have it installed right away." The butler continued. "I will let someone carry your luggage. Please follow me."

The moment she steps in the first thing she notices was the flooring that utilized maple. It is a developed polyurethane floor finishes made hardwoods. This contributed graze- and scratch-resistance to the wood, while also providing a moisture-resistant block to leaks and damp soles. After few steps see notice, the center hall flooring is a Roman Mosaic with Polychrome patterns. Some type of wax that she cannot say for now should have polished this.

Then she glances up on the high ceiling house. Lavish cut-crystal chandeliers hanging from the wide hall surprise her. "That is so old but remarkable!" she cannot stop whispering on her inside.

This defines wealth maintain from decades or even some century.

Uncomfortable Attention

"It is overwhelming when you are not used to surprises."

After the savage meal of pure pleasantry, she is now inside the huge room that was double the size of her apartment with the modern interior design with minimal display of white and gray. Something is up in her mind. Something that she cannot say for now. To her surprise, the design that she had on her desk that nearly no one knew about was in front of her. This is the exact room of her dream. From the tiniest bits of detail was followed.

It was exactly the lay-out and list of furniture that she has on her mind to own after she finally decided to leave the current unit that she own in NYC.

The detail from the curtain down to the type of mattress on the bed. Is this a kind of a joke? She decided to talk to the CEO.

After the third, ring the man answer, "Hey Sweetheart, Enjoying yourself in the mansion?"

"Joe, is this kind of a joke? Are you kidding me? What is this?" literally her screaming.

"Hang on. What are you talking about? Is there something wrong?" The serious tone of the man.

"Joe, first they gave me a car, license, and now my dream room? What's next?"

"Ah- Darling, that I do not know. I was told to give them information to make you comfortable in your stay there and that is what I provided them. I guess you should be Thankful." This stops her. Joe is a kind of person that would never give wrong information or lies. At least, this drunkard is tested to be honest. It still puzzles her that the detail of the room is in front of her. She never let anyone know about this.

"I'll call you when I have the update on the project. I think I need to make this faster that I thought. That way I can remove myself in this uncomfortable situation." She sighs.

"Alright then. Cheers!"

She lay down on the mattress. "Hang on-Ash, this will be answered when you finally meet this guy."

The battle within her never stops disturbing her. On one note, this could only be a coincident. They maybe are trying to be nice and the designer of the room that she has right now- is of the same taste.

One knock was heard and she rush to open the door.

It was a chambermaid in uniform with the trolley. On top view, you can see the folders and some images. Here it is. It calms her down.

It indeed calms her down seeing that truly she is here to work. Not for the huge hoax, she is feeling deep inside.

"Ms. Dmitri-Parker, here are the files that the Fernsby would want you to see for the project."

"Thank you. I'll take the files from here." She never opens the door wider for the lady. She insisted on taking the files by the door. The girl walks away.

She immediately goes through the files and she found some images. It was an old shack by the river. It was showing her the old picture of the shack when it was still fully furnishing and functional and the current picture of the shack that was renovated but empty interior.

It looks great for her. It would then be easy. She assesses the timeframe and timetable. She can do the overall work within 5 days. She will get the proposal done right now before the meeting then she can let them know about the timetable of her work.

She started on constructing the three best option for the interior of the shack. It will be perfect when she has the presentation up.

Great thing about having the years of experience was the list of fabric, list of plants, list of stones, list of paints, and list of furniture that she can recommend depending on the ideal of the person.

She can tailor fit it to your taste like a seamstress.

Meeting the Who

"Conversation from someone you wouldn't expect…"

Apparently, the meeting appears to be a buffet. There are varieties of food on the long table that is laid out. She was a little formal on the choice of dressing however she bares in her mind that she is not here to party but to do a business proposal.

I was starting to get dark. She is about to sit on the chair next to her assistant however she was guided to another chair near the head of the table.

"The Fernsby mention to let you sit next the head chair." The butler commented.

It will be ideal so they can hear each other. She is about to put her laptop in her lap when another voice stops her. "As the family tradition of the Fernsby, gadgets and electronic will be set aside in the left counter. Food is delicate and needs to be respected." The butler inserted.

When she is done handling all the folders and laptop, there was a voice of a Man who echoed on the room.

"It seems that your details annoy them too- Rodrigo. Give them a break!" a loud husky voice from the aisle. As she laid an eye on the owner of the voice, she notices a muscular mid-30's guy with green eye, curly black hair down to his shoulder, 6'4 ft. tall and divided chin.

As she was expecting the man to sit on the head of the table the person, sit right next to her. It makes her sit right in the middle of this guy and the person who will sit on the head of the table. "Hello, there! I would guess you are Ashley. I'm Ryker Remington Fernsby." the friendly start of the stranger.

"Yes. I was a pleasure finally meeting you Mr. Fernsby." She nervously utters. There was this kind of cool air that covers her lungs right after Ryker speaks. It was weird but it appears that there is a strange aura. She felt fear when she is looking at the eye of the man. The smile of Ryker from his thin lips seems to draw her in to a warmth whimsical shiver. It was fear that she has never felt before. She offers a hand as a formal gesture but was pulled in to a hug.

"We don't do formality here Ashley. I am a hugger." Playful approach of the man. She was forced to smile although the strange feeling is still there. What a dark charmer!

Then when she turns her head on the other side of the table. She was shock not to notice that there is someone already occupying the space.

It was a girl version of the guy that she just hugged. Until their eyes meet, she was drawn in to extreme warmth and lonely feeling. It was weird. What is happening to her?

She found that this lady has hazel nut brown eyes and has a pointier nose. She examines the lady that stunned her and she was drawn to her clothing. It was a formal personalized tailored coat matched with the high waist elegant black slack and white shirt. She was a goddess.

"So, shall we dine?" the lady broke her stare and address the people on the table. She was embarrassed that she was not able to introduce herself to the lady.

"I wish to have a word with you in private about the house tomorrow morning on my study. I believe the blueprint of the house is already given to you by Rod. Please find yourself in by exactly 6 in the morning." The sweetest authoritative voice of the lady with no name.

"Alright, I will." She shyly answered. Apparently, the guy that they are questioning was a woman. If this is the person giving her more direct answer towards the fulfillment of her work, then this must be the person she will work for. She was not expecting the turnout of events. Normally, the boy will sit on the head of the table and the boy will give more business like spirit. It was 21st century after all.

"I want you to first get well rested on the first night with us." The final note of the lady before she digs in her food and turn silently. This lady of the house is giving her a distinctive and pervasive quality in a quirky manner in a dark manner but still hard to resist.

It was remarkable that the chef of the house was able to come-up easily on the meal that would fit her specially that she has lactose intolerance and gluten intolerance. She needs to be very careful on her meal. It is notable that both the host of the house are picking on the same type of meal that she is enjoying. This can be another similarity.

Some of the meal that was present in the dining hall were Creamy Tomato Gluten Free Pasta, Pasta with Broccoli, and Gluten-Free Chicken and Dumplings.

While digging in the food, Ryker stated to initiate a chat. "Great that finally we have someone with the same taste of food. Do you know that we both have lactose and gluten intolerance? It was the first that we have a visitor that wouldn't request for a separate set of meal. Are you enjoying the food?" Is this person reading her mind? Or is this part of the trick that they have? Or maybe she is being too cautious and paranoid. She tried to seek comfort on her secretary however; on her surprise, Victoria is enjoying the company of Rodrigo.

"I am. This day is full surprises. The food looks well prepared." She commented not to go beyond what was running in her mind. There are many thoughts that still pile up for her to get the answer.

"Expected to be well-prepared knowing that the Chef is the first of his class on one of the finest school in England." Strict comment of the lady on her right without even glancing to the people around.

At first, she felt the need to know the lady but because of the cold response she sensed that it would be a little hard. On the other hand, it seems that the lad on her left was giving her attention and effort to get along. This is a complete opposite on the impression that she had couple of minutes ago.

"How was the impression on the country? I believe it was your first time?" the friendly note from the manly tone of Ryker.

"It going alright. New Zealand always has been a home of fun art that I would love to explore. I am a big fan of Tolkien's work." Her response.

"Ah. Then it will be our first Saturday tour destination." Ryker positively note. This statement made her smile. Ryker will join them with the tour. Excitement covers her body right now. She remembers the first work of Tolkien, which is "The Silmarillion". Although it was not the exact details used in the series LOTR, it was the great build-up. That she can say brought the fine extravaganza of the LOTR.

With the exchange of conversation, she had with Ryker the fear he felt for him disappear. He is showing this stares that she cannot say what for. She must admit she is quiet fond of him now.

He has a light soul that can be be-friended. This is the only thing that is for sure.

The conversation between the two becomes naturally pleasant that she did not even notice that the girl is now gone and her assistant is waving at her to say good night.

Chapter Three

"When the inscriptions prime for more queries,
Trying to neglect would never resolve."

The Study Room

"Unexpected glances are sometimes the desire of our soul…"

IT WAS A DELIGHTFUL NIGHT after she established a new friend in Ryker. She was able to enjoy the company of the man. That same night Ryker revealed the name of her twin sister Amanda Desiree. They are both born in Nigeria by the property that their parents had. They stayed for only three years there before moving permanently in NZ. The twins had a different degree. Ryker was into Arts and Craft while Amanda was into Business to retain the decades of family heritage. This should be the reason why she is dealing with Amanda. It would definitely easier if it was Ryker but she cannot choose her Client.

It was the next morning, Ashley walk through the wide hall of the mansion, which feels like the hall of Hogwarts in Harry Potter film. So huge that the walls are not reachable by any ladder. She enjoys the ancestral effect of the huge curtain that makes the hall like a runway of a palace. Although she wanted to ask Ryker about the kind of business their family have for decades, she cannot intrude. As she wanders, she is guided with the map on her hand.

She reached the study and with her being just meters away from the opening- the door open. Therefore, this is sensor activated.

"I am right here. Please feel free to find a sit!" the voice of Amanda coming from the left alley of the study room that looks like a giant library. From her initial observation, this is like her University library. Not to mention this had more limited edition books that a normal shelf probably would not have.

She rested on the long elegant couch in front of the table. Baffled with the set-up, she tried finding the office table that is commonly found in a business transaction however it was like plainly a tea table with soft cushions. There isn't a choice but to sit on the center of the study where there is a couch and small table to sit on. The textile on the flooring is again a mosaic that is seen to be old but never tarnish.

"You are right on time. You might find it easy to follow the map." The voice of Amanda draws nearer until she is of sight. Ashley tried to follow where the voice is coming from while placing the folder and her computer on the table for her presentation.

"It is like a puzzle that I need to solve believe me." She casually started a small talk. "This place is massive." She continued as she was looking around the array of books in their distinctive places.

"This makes you the first person to successfully enjoy the exploration of the mansion." Their eye meets but the lady of the house instantly looks down. "That is- if you enjoy adventure and rules." She finished her statement as she takes a sit on one of the chairs in front of Ashley.

She was able to observe that the formal lady she met last night was plainly in a white oversize shirt covering any undergarments or shorts she may have. She also wonders whether there is something inside the shirt or none. Should I say, the question was focusing more whether this lady had a partner on her bed last night? Some playful thoughts that she keeps on pushing away. This is also noticeable that the girl is walking barefoot around with only a pencil which is keeping her hair up.

"Done criticizing my outfit lady?" she was caught off guard with the sentence of the strict lady. On the other hand, Amanda might not realize that she just walks around in her bedclothes. She always got distracted when she need to read her favorite book- Little Woman to keep her in the chaotic business world.

"I am not criticizing. I am just overwhelming that you can be this casual." Honest response from her. One thing about Ashley, she can't stop her mouth from stating her thoughts. Most of the people find it charming some find it harsh. Depending on the comment of the honest woman.

"Now, you are judging." Amanda blushed without an intent of doing so. It was interpreted in another manner by Ash. The poor girl thought that it was anger but truly, it was shyness.

Ashley come to her senses that she might have offended the client. "I- don't mean any harm. I am speaking my head out. I am sorry." She ducks her head out. While the other woman tried to see the gesture.

Down for Business

"Having the work done fast sometimes lead to having it done long."

Putting aside the shyness, one woman broke the growing silence, "It might be a great ordeal to start discussing about the shack." Amanda tried to direct the conversation on the business agenda. While this statement brought the narrowed eyes of the designer to the eyes of the woman speaking.

Amanda continued, "I am able to supervise the architect and engineer that work on the renovation of the shack. If you can observe on the blueprint, it was no longer a plain wooden house by the river. It is now a modern glass outer rear to adopt the modern design of modern architecture. But interesting enough it was not. Due to the location and how it was fully rested on the dirt by the river." With confidence that the woman state.

This is a great opportunity for the designer to show off her talents and observation. "I am able to notice the I-Beam, Lite block and wood work patterns on the cemented wall." Ashley added trying to catch the interest of the client. "Which is a wise choice knowing the area is by the water?"

"Awesome, I am geeking with you here." Amanda smiles. This is the first time that the stranger from the States is able to notice the affirming response. On the other side, Amanda is so impress that the interior designer has vast knowledge even in Architecture. She might have few units with Architecture the reason she was able to come up with the specific request on the material of the shack.

"Also the mason work on the sharpness of the corners made it really elegant that I wouldn't have a hard time on designing the interior." Ashley pointed on the images on the table with the bare design of the shack. "I might need to see this close up so I can confirm whether the wall is perfect. I might be very meticulous on the wall finishing. I hope you don't mind."

"Not at all. I am glad we are having the same intent. I want everything to be perfect. Seamless if necessary. If I can redo the entire thing, I will." Amanda utters with a smirk. Showing that she is confident in terms of the mason work on each corner of the inner textile.

"I am able to give you the interior lay-out that I wish to adopt here right? It was part of the paper works that I have sent last night." Amanda asked while looking at the lady in front of her which is biting her pen while looking carefully on the images on the table. She was able to check how the complexion of Ashley shines more when the sun is hitting her. She never sees a different glow on common American. This have established questions on her mind. The moment Ashley motion to look at her, she manage to draw her sight on the other direction.

"Yes, I am suggesting using this minimalist design." Ashley handed Amanda two sets of folder. Keeping another two sets in her hand just in case the first two does not work.

Amanda lean back to the single Victorian couch and lies her head in the soft cushion. This shift of movement made her shirt expose some of her skin. Ashley's curiosity got answer when her eye involuntarily run through the long trunk until her eyes fall on the woman's girdles. Not a single mark of imperfection! She tried to remove her eyesight on the royal blue Fleur of England undergarment. But for her it was too late, she was able to venture her eyes on the parts that satisfy her curiosity.

A voice brought her back to reality. "I am glad you did your modification on the template that I gave you. I like the second option with the extended garden effect. This will make me think that I am just walking through the hall then not realizing I am already in the garden." Amanda lowered the folder and shows an affirmation.

Ashley is like a boiling pot that the steam is getting out of her ear. Her face is fully red and her ear. "Are you okay?" the question of the Kiwi.

"I am alright. Just nervous that you wouldn't like any of the designs." She hid the real reason that she does not understand herself. "H-how did you achieve the corner of the glass wall in the exterior if we are just using an I-Beam?" Curious note of the interior designer while watering her drying throat out of shame.

On the other hand, this made Amanda boast on her innovative ideas. "I have the two I-beam shave off its head and linking them together." Amanda look at the eye of the designer.

The stare almost lasted couple of seconds which is uncomfortable for the Kiwi. After not getting any response, she decided to redirect her stare and asked, "How long can we have this done?" It is strange that every time they stare at each other there was either burst of emotion of nervousness inside her.

"Give me five full days." Ashley tries to give the fastest time she can had this done. This is a quick answer after the tension of the stare brought her to her silence.

"I may need to let you know that I can't give you the full day. The river where the shack is located is also a place where an orphanage resides nearby. I have given the garden as recreational activities for the children to roam around." Amanda utters concern about the American's timetable. "Will it be safe to say- 5 hours in a day?" Ending statement of the Kiwi.

"I am not mistaken the shack is just adjacent to the mansion right? So, the orphanage is also nearby?" The question of the American to get the affirmation of the Kiwi.

Amanda nod as a response.

"I now understand as to why I am given a month here." Ashley state in low voice hoping that the client would not hear.

Pleasant Interruption

"Kind eyes see the soul and see satisfaction more easily."

With her arrival at the manor in the middle of the Week-Wednesday, she was able to visit the shack for two days. With her tools and assistant, they are able to assess the readiness of the shack. The weekend after was a magical weekend with the Habbiton tour with Ryker.

The lad has become part of her day and something that she will search whenever he was not around. This is an undeniable growth of affection between the two. There are many free hours knowing that the garden is jump pack during the kid's hour as she calls it.

A week well spent, she was able to get the two bedroom fixed and the kitchen furnished. Although it would take her another week finishing the entire kitchen alone due to the fine detail that Amanda gave her, it did a fulfillment to know she is almost done with the project. She is currently in the garden arranging some outer décor to make it appealing for the client.

After the last conversation they had on the study, she never had a glimpse of the woman again. According to Ryker as the priestess, she had the obligation to the vestry. She cannot understand it fully when Ryker was a huge humorous guy that you can't identify which is true and not. Would this mean that the girl is a religious align head as well aside from the fact that she is the head of the Fernsby's business? She did a well verse research in the family background of the Fernsby due to the intriguing chill it brought her. Then she notices that the empire was rarely featured in the news and magazine. It was stated that the billionaire family are too private and media are off limits. Imagine how high this info triggered her. Even the president of the United States is not immune to the media yet this family made it just as cool as 100 years.

She tried to ask on the chambermaid and they said that the lady of the house is in Scotland for business meeting and will be back by Wednesday Night. Fair enough because she will need opinion on the progress of the work.

Ryker was not a help as well even the lad is always with her in her work. Sometimes he is a destruction and sometimes refreshment. She can see her bubbly dad in this guy.

She was about to move a pot of monstera around when a ball hit her back. "Ouch!" She immediately turns and look around. There she spotted a tiny boy running towards her with a nearly teary eye. This boy has a rare eye color. His left eye was a shade of blue and gray while the other was a green nearly brown. This makes the boy attractive for her. How can she be mad?

"I-ii am s-sorry. I didn't mean to hit you." It was the cutest voice from a more likely 4-6-year-old toddler.

She levels down to the height of the boy. "It is all right. It does not hurt. What are you doing here alone?"

"I always play here when nobody's around. The other kids don't like to play with me." The sad tone of the little child.

"Why is that? Do you want to share?" She sits down to the newly built swing just adjacent to the back entrance of the shack. She motions the child to sit down along with her.

"They call me freak Miss. You see I have this weird eye and a huge mass at the back of my shoulder." That was the time that she was able to see the huge lump on the back of the child. There is a sting in her heart when the child shows great sadness upon telling her.

"You know what. I don't think that you are a freak. To tell you, your eyes are gorgeous and that mass on your back is something that the doctor can remove." She utters hope to the child.

The child smile and look at her deeply. She was sudden with the action of the child when he hugged her. "Miss, thank you. You are the second person to say that." Wondering who the first was.

"What is your name?" She inquired.

"When I was brought here I am given no name. But my friend calls me Bob." The response of the innocent angel in front of her.

"If you want, you can play here at this hour to make sure that I will be around. The river is not safe for you without someone watching." She offered the child. Wondering why this was the only time that she saw the poor kid.

"Thank you. I think I need to go. The social worker might not like me going beyond the time they have allotted." The child run leaving his ball on the swing.

She watches the child go through the bushes and disappear. There be surely another meeting for them both. She kept the ball in the corner of the sofa.

She watches the child go through the bushes and disappear. She has a soft spot for children more of the thought the child was just like her-Orphan. How the turn of events in her life was the not how it usually goes for someone who lost their parents at a young age. More of it was just luck. More of it was a blessing she doesn't deserve.

Remembering the part of her life when she tried to get an academic scholarship yet never got in because of the lack of paper document for the said fulfillment of the scholarship. One of the complication led to another as she was incapable of financing her own tuition fees. Then after a week of crying as a surrender, a call from the university came and mention, the 4-year program paid in advance for her to take. The mysterious person still remains a mystery. As she tried to get a contact detail it was just a hired P.O Box somewhere in Canada was given. It was a great chance for her to pass so she took it. Every time, she sends gifts and letters for her sponsor and in return after graduation- she received the painting that was in her home office with the note.

The note mention- "I hope when time comes you can return the favor." Without hesitation, she is willing to pay for her debts. Money is a great affliction in her life, but now that her stability was sealed, she can give her entire savings just to show gratitude on the person that pay off her life ahead.

Then an alarm coming from the orphanage brought her back to reality. It has been awhile she is in the shack. Rodrigo and Victoria are in the shopping spree for the kitchen and will be back soon. Seems that it would take time for them to be back.

Chapter Four

The Others

*"When feelings are the basis for an action, a lot will surely complain.
But how will it turn if the feeling is accompanied with evidences?"*

Gentle Touch

"Easily broken, easily healed."

SOMEONE ENTERS THE SHACK WITH medieval clothing- layers of elegant dark red and black fabric stating volume and rank. Underclothes covered with an underskirt made of dark red linen or silk with of breeches, chemise and hose. The medieval robe covering the head of the individual makes it easy for any identity to be hidden to plain sight. It was unexpected that the area would open knowing it is guarded. Not unless, there is someone inside.

There is this unexplained force of the movements of the trees and the whisper of the air to the entities ear stating, "Drew closer…"

This feeling come out strong, as the high sense of smell of the invader whiffs an unusual scent as the person approach the shack. "This can't be. Don't tell me she is here." The inner voice of the intruder. With this certainty and excitement, the heart of the invader beat on top of its capability. The familiar scent that dance in its nose made some worry on its heart. "What is she doing here this late?"

With careful steps, the individual enters the renovated abode that was looking glamorous although obviously not completed yet. It come to the attention of the invader that someone has fully rested on the couch. It was the woman. It is confirming. The desire of the intruder heightens. The longing to touch her or be near her makes the intruder's heart skip its beat.

She looks fitting in the entire place. The special force draws the person to bend and sit right next to the charming lady. Examining the entire being of the lady, it reaches to the strand of hair that is hiding the perfect face of the woman. As the gesture makes the woman release a soft moan of acceptance, the stranger smiles.

"Such a charmer! I hope you will choose us." utterance that was unexpected to escape the lips of the intruder. A gentle stroke of hand smoothly caresses the cheek of the sleeping woman...

It made the day of the stranger then decided to walk away.

Ashley was able to feel a gentle touch on her face and able to hear the soft utterance. Weird as it might sound, the feeling of having someone gently place its hand on her face doesn't feel disturbing. The warmth of the soft hand cradles her to a secure company. As she forces herself to open her eyes, she saw a blur image of the back of a person with a cloak leaving the area. She tried to call the stranger, "Wait!" With much effort, the voice came out like a whisper. It clearly didn't call the attention of the stranger who is walking away. Because of the long day, she was not able to make an effort to confirm if it was a work of her imagination or a dream. She then decided to give it to her heavy eyes and continue sleeping.

Victoria and Rodrigo was near the renovated shack accompanied with the hardware personnel who's carrying the supply. The beautiful half-black American-Cuban strides the fine grass. Then it caught her attention that the door of the shack is open at this hour without any lights on. She looks at her Chanel limited edition watch on her wrist. Nine in the evening. This worries her.

"Do you receive any information from Ashley about her whereabouts?" Rodrigo asked Victoria. Then Rodrigo beep his electronic watch and send a signal to his security team on the area.

"She didn't use her car meaning she should be here somewhere." The woman started to express worry. "She should have opened the lights if she is inside." Vicky seek assurance to the butler as they stare at each other.

"I'll go inside first and stay back till I am able to confirm that the area is safe." Rodrigo fasten his phase and in no time reached the porch. The man is already in a surveillance mood automatically as he rises its protective weapon.

She tried to make some bigger step although the heels that she wore is not allowing her to do so. The woman's heartbeat is deafening. She doesn't know how to react if the woman isn't safe on her watch.

Then, Rodrigo's voice broke out, "She's here on the couch." Makes her heavy feeling go away. Then the butler opens the light.

Ashley is making a remarkable job on this project like the other projects that she handled. It was an honest feedback from a co-worker. This lady had the highest standard you she has encountered in terms of design. Which made her name one of the highest paid designer in the company. Now that she is looking at the sleeping girl-, she remembers that after all she is still an ordinary person. Need some rest… Need some sleep…

"Should we call it a day? It was beyond the time. As per agreement, you guys can only work 5 hours but since last week you are working 6-7 hours." Rodrigo's reaction while looking at the sleeping boss.

"How casual we are today Rodrigo? Seems that my charms are getting in to you, finally." She tried to hit on the person again. In addition, sway her hip to bump the guy intentionally.

"You should know that I also have limits. Be careful, one day, I might take your jokes seriously." Quick utterance of the guy.

This reaction somehow confused the humorous girl. "Ey? Man problems- when will you take me seriously. Seeing ladies as jokes." She responded in a lower tone.

"What?" Rodrigo asked. Wondering what does the funny American said.

"Nothing." She now motions to wake Ashley when just in time she was stop by the butler.

"One thing about your culture that I personally don't agree on is waking a person up. I would just carry her and if we succeed she can have a good long sleep in the manor."

She must admit. She is liking the culture of the Kiwi or is this only true to this man.

The Council

"Darkness is mostly feared but mostly used for weary soul."

In the chamber which is fatally deep khronal dark and virulent dreary red-bricked, stand a circle of people standing on the obnoxious place.

"How can you be sure that she will agree to this?" Redhood scream to the crowd. After the said statement there are small whispers within the 12 other head priest. "She barely knew you and smelling her scent doesn't make any sense." The protesting man spit in front of the other head priest.

"Don't disrespect the imperial priest! You don't have any rights." Blacklord warn the protesting man. From the stinging stare of each of the high priest, the others remain silent not until…

"Wees seën oor u twyfel. Ek twyfel ook. Maar ons moet probeer." (Be bless on your doubt. I doubt it too. But we need to try.) The sinister voice of the imperial priest resonates.

The dark room in the hidden hollow of the manor somehow lit up when a hush of air with fire exposed itself when the voice of the powerful priest echoed the entire room.

"There is no other option but to try. The book states that we can all be healed by a true pure born." The imperial priest adds on. "Only once in a century. Down with one century. Give hope to try. Some of us was able to witness the previous heir of the century as they failed. Who can really say that we will succeed? Who can say we will lose? We need to try." The whispers now disappear as the tone of the simple words run through the hall. They are well aware that the power of the imperial priest was beyond they have combined. It was known when the birth of the moon becomes the death of the sun.

Silverwand then state, "You are well aware that the ritual must be conscientious."

"I am"

"How can you make her agree with the limited time? She will leave before the new moon." The query of Redhood.

"Blacklord was tasked for that."

"glo" (Have faith) Blacklord chant.

"geloofsbroer hê" (Have faith brother) chant of the others.

After the chants of the twelve other high priest, the imperial priest stayed on the chamber, which is connected, to one of the secret room. It sits a huge desolated area, which is positioned, below the Royal Waterways. The imperial priest looks at its own reflection.

"I am sure about you. I am sure since I encountered you in the comfort room of your university." Then it recites the Prophesy of the Awakening, "The tears that drops turn into joy, my challenge to heal us both." It was the first sign that the high priest encountered. It was also the full awakening of the gift of the deprecor. The visions, nature calling, super heighten senses starts when the person encounter Ashley.

This is the reason why the scholarship of Ashley was paid in full. The main reason why no one can harm her and can go near her. Ashley is fully guarded the entire time. With seven attempt of drunk people going near her, with three robberies on her apartment, two project sabotage all of these are securely fixed by the high priest. Rodrigo was already with her for eight years.

With the chants there is someone awakens from her deep sleep. How strange it is that she is hearing the conversation of a forum in her dreams. She is still hearing the voices of chants. A language that she cannot understand. "What the heck is wrong with this house that she started to hear voices?"

The Encounter

"It arrives when it was uninvited."

Because of the disturbing voices that she heard from her dream, she decided to make a coffee on the chambermaid's kitchen. Everyone is asleep at least what she thinks of. She is now sitting on the counter tops and is about to sip on the coffee when one voice from the nook of the kitchen speaks, "Nightmares?" serious unusual tone from a man.

"Ryker? You scared the hell out of me." Her reaction while touching her sternum to control her heartbeat.

"My apologies. I did not mean to scare you." Ryker continue with the deep serious tone.

"Yes, nightmares. I can say that." That is what she wanted to think of at least. "What are you doing here yourself?"

"I cannot sleep. But nothing important." Hearing the serious tone from the man scare her. "Would you want to talk about the nightmare?"

"Ryker, this situation still confused me. How'd you get the information about me? I mean… this situation spooks me. It all started with a car then with a room which is my dream room what would be the next?" Ashley expressing so emotional giving it away that the nightmare bothers her.

"I don't know how to respond to that. For I didn't know you have issue with our hospitality." Ryker utters slowly making sure not making the girl feel more terrible.

"I am glad for this project don't get me wrong. I do not have issue with you nor the project. It is hard for me to understand that all this is coincidental," the girl explained.

"Then maybe it isn't. Maybe it was a sign from the Universe that you need to listen. Are you happy on nearly the end of the project?'

"Yes." The girl was able to calm down now. She took a sip of coffee she prepared. As she does so, the person look at her deeply. "What do you mean a sign from the Universe?"

The guy looks like he was taken a back from the question, "Never mind me. I do have this eccentric belief that no one can dive in. I don't want to bore you." The boy looks at the other side, "Will you share what kind of dream upset you?"

"It is weird. I feel like I am inside a dark room with twelve people whose wearing all different dark shaded robe. Ancient Robes! It looks like they are shaman or anything whimsical. They are talking about someone that they need to convince to-" before being able to continue Ryker release a weird laugh.

"That was really weird. I think you need to rest well, sweetie. You are just tired. Although, it would have been great to dream of me." The guy wink at her. "All I can say. If the room is not comfortable to you, I can let you move to the next room of your liking. We have more than 20 rooms. You can choose one."

The girl just looks at the hand of the man who is holding her hand right now. It was a comforting touch. She had no experience with this kind of closeness to anyone. She retrains herself for a long time but then his man can easily go beyond her boundary.

"This house tells story of all our heritage. If you are scared to stay with us, you just need to ask." The man added.

"I am not complaining. I am scared." The man releases her hand from his soft grip.

"What are you scared of?"

"That the comfort that this place is too much. I am scared that I felt instantly close to the place. Even with the dreams lately…"

"Isn't it great. That was a compliment for us. It was not the place that you are scared. It is yourself. New Zealand is not bad."

Then the lady was drawn to think of what the guy state. She needs to try this place. This will make her soul more peaceful. Then her eyes landed on the guy's footwear. It made her eyebrow flick. Where does this guy hike at this late hour? His shoes are full of mud. Not her business…

She just neglected it and tried to find a courage to start a talk. "Where were you the entire day?"

"So, we are growing emotions? Missing me? "The feedback of the man although the tone is still down.

"Don't flatter yourself too much just not used to entire day of working wonderfully without someone bugging me." She flushed the redness on her face when the confidence of the man overthrown hers.

"It was going well Missy then you killed it again. Literally no idea of how flirting goes." The direct voice of the man.

"Are we?" She then asked.

"I clearly need to exert more effort for you to realize? I figured my indirect charm would not work. How about trying the blunt approach?" This had the girl drop her jaw and froze.

With that statement the guy approach her. The tall guy towered over her and left only few inches away from her face. She was able to see the dark stare of the man. This is not the bubbly guy that she grew affection on. She reaches to the nearest object she can seek refuge on. However, was trap in the broadness of the man, she felt extremely caught in the act and don't know what to do.

"I am not rushing Ashley. I am very ancient and I can wait. I can wait." Probably the man notices her reaction. Then walk swiftly like a royal blood down the foyer of the room and turn left to the main hall until the shadow is no longer visible.

"Is he for real? I haven't-" then she remembers the everyday meal that the man offers to her. He is making and baking them himself. All the attention that he is giving.

Can this be his gentle way of flirting and letting her know that he likes her? But there is something that she is seeing in the eye of the man. A forceful action that was not done willfully. How can she identify it if her lack of experience on this area stand her way?

———————◆━✕━◆———————

Chapter Five

The Moon

"With the beauty that was borrowed, will the eye of innocence see the deeper sense?"

The Talk

"Senses are the main cause of fear."

I T WAS PAST 2 AM. Exactly an hour after the conversation she had with Ryker. Feeling confused she decided to stroll over the huge garden adjacent on the shack that she is working on and the other building which should be the orphanage.

Nights as troublesome for her. Nightmares that she always experiences since childhood. But somehow she learned how to value and see the beauty of the outdoor scenery. She is a kind of person that will not easily got scared by a dark nook or alley.

The night was magical because of how the moon shines above the nearby lake. It makes a fascinating reflection of the moon on the water where she is looking over. "Mom, I am hoping you can hear me. I wish to get advices on a lot of things." As she was uttering those words, she holds on to her pocket and tried to get the bracelet that her mom gave her on her 3rd birthday. Not that she can remember her mom giving it to her, but her aunt was able to keep it until she come of age.

She raises it up and try to make it shine through the brightness of the moon. She then touches the half crescent moon on the charms of the bracelet. "I don't want to be alone throughout my life. I know mom. It was the opposite on the statement I told Aunt Liza. But should I entertain Ryker? Should I let him get into my heart?". There was a stillness of the surrounding leaving the crickets sound and the air be the melody of the night.

Then, there was a noise on the bushes that made her turn and search for the source.

"Who's there? Reveal yourself." She holds on tight to her bracelet and try to look for the pocket knife that she always brings along. Then the sound of the bushes becomes louder. She is now certain that it was from her right. She prepared her stance for she expects an immediate attack from the bushes.

Out of nowhere a figure appear and spoke, "I am sorry, Miss. I am wondering around then I spotted you." It was a tiny familiar voice from the child. It was Bob. As he reveals himself to the lady on a visible distance.

"What are you doing here Bob? It is so late." The lady kneels down after feeling relief from the unexpected encounter.

"The moon is something that I always like to watch. Isn't it wonderful?"

"It is. I always talk to my mom through the moon. I felt like she is near me when I am staring at it." She slowly commented on the response of the child.

"Do you know that my friend also likes the moon?" the response of the child. It was not the first time that the child mentions the friend that he has.

"I am now curious on who is your friend."

"You will meet soon." The boy holds her and gave her a charming smile. "I need to go" the boy come out running toward the bushes again. Then he turns around, "You will not be alone, Miss. You will never be alone." She wished to call for the child and at least lead him back to the facility however the child was quick enough to be chased.

In no time, boy disappears within the bushes and trees. The child intrigues her so much. She promises that after the contract that she had here. She will inquire to the orphanage if she can possibly adopt the child. She's been thinking about adoption from quite some time now.

"How weak the security of the orphanage here." The inner voice of the woman as she attests the security of the orphanage. In the states, it would never be possible for young orphan to wander around in this late hour.

She decided to walk towards the shack. Why not give it a little visit?

The cool air blows as the trees sway. Such a beautiful place! The lone thing she thinks of when looking at the view.

The Shadow

"When the whisper of eager soul was heard by the granting spirit, gifts and provision will come flooding."

On the other side of the garden there was someone watching the brightness of the moon. The individual was known to be the high priest of the Pansélinos Wiccan Group. They believe on the spirit and holiness of the environment.

Best practices of respect and witch craft is there aim. It was forbidden to kill any life with soul. Rumor has it that they are an evil cult. Whereas the truth they are just like the other religious group. They don't believe in one definite name but they believe in the power of the Universe.

The curse that has been cast was from a woman of the opposite tribe hundreds of years ago. It was due to the accident that leads to the death of her child in the hands of the Panselinos Wiccan Tribe.

According to the legend of the family, it was the high priest of that generation who tried to heal the sickly child. The child was defiant and monstrous that the other tribes wish to vanish the child from the land. Fernsby's Great Grand Father tried to heal the child by taking it to this custody for a water ritual. However, as it was the end of the water ritual, the poor child drawn in front of the mother.

The mother curse the entire Tribe. The curse as her cast was to let the elders and distant relations of the Fernsby to live and never sleep until the True Pure born will come to love the heir of the Fernsby. Marriage under the Blood moon and first consummation with full consented love.

It sounds so easy to find the breaker of the curse at first however to decipher the code given by the word true pure born is beyond any books. Aside from the curse of no sleep and not dying, the Fernsby suffers from shape shifting every 3 am until 4 am. This would show their rotten image that would reveal their century old age. This needs to be accepted by the True Pure Born.

The night of the blood moons. The palm of the two heir and the breaker of the curse will light as bright as the moon. It was the only sign that can identify if Ashley is truly the key to the awakening.

Every thought played in the mind of the high priest. The high priest is aware that the woman is wondering around as they can sense and feel the movement of the woman even from a far.

"Four Years ago as I am watching you sleeping on your room Ashley. I already know that even I fail or even the curse will not break I would be happy to spend eternity if you will choose me. I didn't mean to drag you to this mess. How I wish I am just an ordinary human born at this century." The high priest utters as the true image of age come to its skin.

"Who are you?" The priest heard the question of Ashley from a far. It also sudden the individual.

"Can you hear me?" As the individual tried to ask the woman from its location.

"Where are you? Why am I hearing you on my head?" the woman releases a tiny laugh "Maybe I am just being insane. Great this place made me lose my mind."

"Oh no. You didn't. You will understand soon. This is also new to me. But it is a good thing. Just call me and I will be your company."

There was a long silence that the priest worry for the woman on the garden.

"I have one question. Are you a werewolf or a vampire? Are you my mate or sort of?"

"H-hahah. You are full of Science Fiction on yours shelve that it gets in your brain. I am neither a vampire nor a wolf. But you can be my mate." The individual play around to lighten up the mood as the sense of hearing was certain that the heartbeat of the woman is beyond the normal speed.

"Then reveal yourself." This statement brought the exchange they are doing to an end. The priest can't reveal how rotten it's physical appearance this moment to the woman.

"Soon, love. Soon." Soon when the high priest is certain that the woman can handle the reveal and the shift that they had. Certainty that she will not suffer from heat attack.

High Priest

"Taking chances on the wheel that you drive, will lead you on direction you choose."

"Ashley!" she felt another nudge on her arm. "Ashley, you over slept. It is already 12 noon and the Fernsby are waiting in the dining hall. You skip the breakfast and we are worried as to what happen to you." The voice become clear as the woman open her eyes.

It was her secretary on a casual clothing. "Why did you wake me up just now? If you are that worry, you should have entered the room this morning." The unexpected utterance that she throws to the other person on the room.

She is even shock by herself too.

"Ah. As if you would value me waking you. Even this idea of doing it right now was not good." Vicky is about to walk out of the room when Ashley catch her wrist and pull her back.

Feeling regretful Ash uttered, "I am sorry." Then the lady holds her painful head. "I am not really in a good shape. There are a lot of things going on." She shared her emotion sincerely without oversharing the details that she rather keeps private.

"I understand. Are you okay?" the friendly girl tried to check on her as she sits down the bed.

"I am. I think I need to rest for today. We don't have a schedule today anyway. We have done the installment on the sink yesterday. We are all up to date. I will just need you to run some errands for me."

"No problem at all. I am able to see your overworking and pushing yourself on the limits. You even skip meals this week."

"Thank you. For the lunch as you said, I wish to politely decline them."

"I will inform them. You don't need to go down. You rest."

She is always thankful with the extremely compassionate heart of her friend. It is rare to find such level of understanding.

She tried to bury her head on the soft pillow and tried to remember last night's event. She wonders as to whether it was product of her imagination or a dream.

How would it be possible for someone to speak to her mind?

"Are you ill?" the voice on her mind stated. Making her jump out of the bed. She tried to check on the area to make sure it was not in the room.

"Your heartbeat scares me? I can't tell you to be calm because this situation and skill is new for the both of us." Addition of the voice.

"Why can I hear you? Can you explain this to me?" Ashley tried to inquire for answers.

"As the season change, another season starts. We offer the spirit of the nature rituals as a sign of thanksgiving on the passing of season and a welcoming ritual for the new season." She continues to listen on the calming voice of the individual. Although, it is difficult to identify the voice. She can't associate the voice to anyone at this point.

"We get to have wishes as the gift of the spirit. For the past year, I keep on wishing a bridge for our soul to unite. I would take this skill as an answer." This brings more question to her mind.

"I am hearing your sigh. Go on then. Ask away." The encouragement of the voice.

"Why are you certain that I am someone you wish for? I am not from here. You don't know me."

"I know you Ashley. I watched you cry and laugh throughout the years."

"You mention last night. You watched me sleeping four years ago?"

"Yes. I have known you long before that."

"This is scary. You sound like a stalker or obsessed individual." The honest opinion of the lady.

"I can't explain further for now. I wish to tell you the details in person. How are you feeling?"

"I feel dizzy."

"I do feel the same this morning. I guess some works of this skill."

She was able to think of one way to force the mysterious individual to show up. She needs to tease it up to lead it to this room.

"You there?" she asked.

"Here always."

"You mention you'll do things for me?"

"Anything."

"Do you know where I am?"

"Yes."

"Can you come over?" After the utterance there was a moment of silence. Then, she gave up. She can't lure the person to reveal that easy.

She sighs and close her eyes.

"I am here." The familiar voice whisper in her ear.

The Answer

"People whom serve with passion will always be rewarded with joy of chances."

The emotion on Vicky as the conversation ends with Ashley as not light. Sometimes she felt ignored by her friend. But that can be understood knowing the woman is not feeling well right now. Then as Vicky go through the dining hall she then announced the absence of the woman and the reason. It was just time that the two Fernsby stand and go through their individual study.

It was her and her new friend who are left on the table. "Rodrigo, we need to go through the list of task for the shack today. I hope you don't mind at all?"

"I am here to help you." The man answered.

"Ashley was never this out of focus in the job. I know that you will disagree on that opinion because you are seeing how dedicated and the quality of work she is doing on the shack but she is really disturbed." The worried individual was digging in the meal prepared for them to share.

"I do see that but it is expected. Knowing she will play a great role in the next coming days." The butler uttered which confused the assistant.

"Bruh! You creepy as f." the instant reaction of the woman.

"There is no point on hiding. You both are here for a reason. Not exactly you but Ashley. I have been watching Ashley since her college days." The woman was having a difficulty on swallowing the food on her mouth.

"I am asked to make her safe by the high priest. Have you heard of the Britain Traditional Witchcraft?"

"Not that it matters on interior design. Does it?" The innocent question of the woman.

"You are funny. I and the Fernsby are part of an inner circle of our cavern. My family has been serving the Fernsby for centuries. When the curse was cast on them, my family are included. Every person you encounter here in the manor was already beyond an ordinary person's age."

"Then, how old must you be?" The tone of a person entertains by the story which is made up by the man.

"Over 200 years old. I lost count some years ago."

"I am 198 years old then." The woman comment before bursting into laughter.

"I am serious. If you have made a research on the creation of a much early Wiccan group, you will encounter Gardner. That man was our last person to enter our group. After he did some chances on the rituals and align it with other pagan works, we stop letting other people enter the cavern." The serious note of the man. "I am telling you these because you might want to leave before it reaches to the point of you not being able to go back to the States."

"If I will be with you, then, my fate is here." Flirtatious comment of the girl without the full believe on the secret being told. "What do you mean you have been watching Ashley?"

"I am. I am able to secure her from any harm. Even from some dangerous drunkard on the road or robbery on her apartment. I am also aware of your full identity as we made an in-depth study near her." The information keeps on coming.

"Let us say... I believe you. What is in Ashley that made you watch her? She is the person we believe will save us from this curse."

"Ashley is purely ordinary. How can see be someone who can save you?"

"You wish not to know. For after that, you are bound to swear filthy to the cavern." The end notes of the guy.

On the other side of the table, the girl continues of eating as she was just laughing at the information she heard. She never took these seriously. She will enjoy sharing this crazy information to her friend.

Chapter Six

Revelation

*"The thrill of meeting someone that deep inside you
desire is the answer for a patient heart."*

Touch of the Wind

*"Resistance is a waste of time, a killer of joy for
someone who wants the roll of the dice."*

AFTER HEARING THE FAMILIAR VOICE at the back of her ear, she felt
anxious as to maybe the person she is going to face is dangerous.
At the same time, this is also a confirmation that she is not going crazy
and not creating some personality on her head. She is uncertain as to
how she felt about this after the internal debate.

Although hesitant, she decided to face the person who is leaning
on her as she was lying down on the bed. Then she saw a familiar eye,
melting her in the deepness of both worry and hopes. She can read the
worry that the eyes are speaking. The person is worrying that acceptance
would be hard for her. As she examines their position which is awkwardly
just inches apart, the person was not anticipating her rush turn.

She felt the deep breath of the individual. As the air of the exhale tingles her skin, there is this comfort and connection that no books can define. She felt the instant connection to the individual. This is unusual but her heartbeat was now relaxing and can say on a normal rate. She was not sure as to how she manages to calm herself down with this strange encounter.

She notices the shaking lips and cheek of the person. She instantly reaches towards the cheek of the person without thinking further on her motion. And asked, "Why are you shaking?" while her eyes landed on the movement she is waiting on the lips of the person in front of her.

"I fear this moment for years that you would run away right after who'd know my presence." The person keeps her palm unto the face. Making sure that Ashley was aware that her touches has a good effect on the person, the individual release some soft moan.

"I felt fear towards this whole trip and I think I ran out of it." She then realizes that this is a no ordinary situation she is in. For the person whom she always saw the shadow some years ago and the person in front of her is another- Woman.

It is Amanda.

The high priestess of the cavern and the person whom will try to break the curse of the entire generations to come. That at least is without her knowledge.

"Why reveal yourself now? If I have felt your presence long before?" Ashley tried to lift herself up to the headboard of the bed and tap the side of the bed for the lady of the manor. This serves a positive invitation for the woman to sit near her. This would be the first time that the New Yorker has someone on her bed.

"I am scared and the whole tribe was waiting for the right time. They wouldn't accept you to the tribe if I haven't seen more evidence of our connection. Those has grown stronger this year." The statement of the lady as she settles next to the girl.

"I don't understand."

"There are much to know." Amanda reaches for the hand of Ashley. This made the other woman look at their locked hands. "I will tell you all the things you wanted to know."

"You are my sponsor. Right?" Ashley being fairly blunt express her theories which has taken Amanda by surprise.

"Yes. I am. How did you know?" Amanda was deeply impress by her senses.

"I saw the signature on the painting that you mention once that you made on the library. It was the same signature that you gave me on my graduation with the letter" She is somehow seeing affirmation on the eye of the woman. As she continues, "This room- this room is the design I have on my office table at home and ship to you."

"Fair enough. Very well! Yes, if you should remember one incident in your college time when you got denied on the University, you run to the comfort room. You are weeping and cursing about how will you make it in. Then you tore one sketch and plan that you made for your dream house." Amanda gave her some more information.

"I remember that. So, you are the one who offered me a make-up kit and towel to freshen up?"

"Yes, I felt your heartbeat starting on that day. It gave me wonders and gifts. I am sure that you are the one right from that moment." The curve on the forehead of Ash made Amanda explain further. "We have high senses once the power of the nature finally come in us and become one of us. Then you come up standing and storming out of the comfort room and neglected my initial interaction. But I saved the house plan, it has notes that was scribbled at the back. Then, I know it was both you and your mom's dream house."

"I comeback for it but never recover it."

"No need because you are already able to make it real. The shack is yours. The shack of your dream." Then Ashley realize the entire house was indeed her mom's ideal house. It was the same sketch and design she used to get in to the University.

"I don't deserve all of this kindness." She knows this is not going to be free. "What do I need to do to repay all your goodness?"

"Marry me." The lady of the manor was too forward on her request knowing that she was left with only one week and a half before the one shoot of a night to break the curse.

"So, that was the whole reason of me being here? To marry a complete Stanger?" Although deep in the heart of the American she never really felt it that way. She was denying herself with the safe and deep connection she felt with the Kiwi. "I didn't even know whether I like girls. This is tough."

"I can't put my objection but I need to let you know about all of this before you answer." The Kiwi dropped her sight on the thick comforter laying on the bed. And on the site where the American was not able to glimpse, shed a drop of tear. This is what she fears. This exact rejection from the woman whom she grown affection throughout the years of watching her from a far and from the dark corner of her room.

This action of Amanda pinches the heart of the woman in front of her. She tried to hid it but deep inside she wanted to just throw her guard off. She was dearly attracted the woman from the moment she saw her. But she hasn't come to the point to ask herself if this can grow to something special and deeper. This would be a lifetime commitment. What worries her is that she doesn't understand what is this whole charade of whimsical ideal that the lady is implying.

"I-I have the whole day to listen to your explanation. Can you first clarify as to what are you?" Ashley left this specific question out.

"I am the head priestess of my cavern. I am a witch. I am gifted to break the curse that put our family and dear friends into suffering. We never age, never sleep, and never die unless we are put into a coffin and tries to starve. We are also shape-shifters. We don't change into any other skin like werewolves but we do show our real skin of age. It was rotten and hideous." Amanda continues to talk without looking at Ashley.

"Witch like Harry Potter?" Ashley inquired.

"Not that kind of witch. We are relying our power from the environmental energy. It was the gift of the spirit of nature. There are wonders that no science can explain."

"What does the curse has to do with me?"

"According to the previous high priest, it would be one person who is my direct equal whom can break the curse- A pure true born."

"So basically, we just need to get married and you are then free from the curse?" Ashley taught it was just simple as that.

"No one really had the understanding on the code that the other witch cast on us. The only thing we understand is we need to get married with your full consent and be with me the complete night till morning of the wedding." Amanda now tries to seek for Ashley's eyes.

"You know. I am not easily scared. I wish to know your shape tonight." Ashley still testing whether this is a made up stories or what.

"As you wish, My love." Amanda utters in a low tone seeing how the situation is hurting her. The woman that she desires. The woman that the moment steps into the mansion she wanted to hug but was not able to do so, is giving her the normal expected resistance. Can't this woman feel the voice of their soul as it clearly ach for every single caresses. Maybe, it would be more ideal for her to leave.

As Amanda was about to stand up, the smaller woman reaches for her wrist and catch her attention. "Can you stay for more? Can you answer all my question now? If I would need to marry you, I need to know you."

This sounds more enlightening to her. At least, the girl is giving it a try.

The Origin of the Curse

"The fruit of a mistaken tragedy."

In the early 15th Century, there was this two big influential family in the Europe. They are believed to be a great source of the power and fair decision. Most of the county people seek council to these families. These two families are close friends. They gather to exchange learnings and celebrations together till one drastic incident happen.

Llewellyn Adelmo Fernsby is the greatest council in the entire county. He is known to be so compassionate and a great provider. All he acquires as evenly shared to all his people. On the other house, the family of equal reputation settles. They are the Villegas.

One secret power of both family is being part of a witchcraft tradition. They both are giving the highest respect to the spirit of the nature. Most known ritual they do was the burning of incense with the delicate ingredients that will give glory to the specific spirits. They are like baking a perfect cake. The power needs to be on the exact measurement.

One night the daughter of Lord Villegas- Laura, knocked on the door of the Fernsby manor. Bringing a new born son covered with a soft mantle hiding his features.

"Laura, such a late time. Get inside!" the kind Lord of the manor let the visitor enters his abode.

"I may need your council and advice on this matter Lord." The woman is tearing up as she uncovered the physique of the new born child.

Then Llewellyn have seen a rare time of deformities. It was a creature without any intact skin. It looks like every layer of the upper skin was burned and rotting. The eye of the child was without a complete eyelid that makes the eyeball exposed like it will fall off. Adding to the rare monstrous feature was a tail and a huge camel like lump on the entire back.

"I beg you my dear Lord. Take him in and do anything to let him heal." Laura is kneeling in front of the lord now and weeping on the state of the son. "My family would let him die without even letting him fight for his life."

"I don't know how we can go about this but I will take him in." The statement of the compassionate Lord to take in some hope on this strange situation.

After some study and a couple of help from the team of physicians on the country, he was able to make the child his own hidden project. He grows love to the innocent child.

Laura was taken by the Villegas and flew her away from the county to leave the people of the county less suspicious about the child.

If this is known by the local people, they would state that the child is curse or demonic. They will surely hunt the said child and butcher it.

This is something that the head of the cavern would not want to happen to any individual of his own circle. He treats Laura as his own child.

His connection of the other county failed to provide his any solution on the deformities of the child. He took on some personal rituals and spells to heal the child. He is leaving the child's progress purely on the wisdom that the spirits are whispering over his ear. In one year the child's skin is already healed. Leaving no touches of the old history and form.

Then on the second year, the child's tail was no longer in question. He was able to cut if off without leading to any complications. Then after another year the eye was also healed. Although it strangely exposed one uniqueness of the child, he was never been happier. The child was able to run and play now. After four nearly five years that the child was just under the hidden passage with the tiny room and toy, he decided to show him the outside to give him the normal life.

The child was with no name. He taught that on Laura's return it would be her right to give the child a proper name.

"Baba, I want to play on the riverbank." The four-year-old boy tries to convince him to go near the water.

"There are a large number of area in the manor to choose from." He doesn't know why the boy wanted to go near the streaming water.

"The light of the sun and the moon radiant more on the water and also the voices of the nature is at highest when I am on the stream." The smart boy speaking like an adult. "Please Baba! I promise to be careful."

"Alright then. You should call your nurse to aid you on the bank." He has not known that it would be his final word to the joyous child.

The next thing that he knows everyone is screaming for help because the child was carried off by the flowing water. By his instinct, he didn't hesitate to jump over the rather deep stream with the extreme current and tries to reach for the child.

He was able to grab the child and swim to the side of the river. As he checks on the child's pulse, a voice from a lady was heard.

"What have you done to my child? I have trusted you his life and you have come a long way to just offer him to the spirit of the water." It was Laura. She is extremely angry.

He never minds the cry of the lady and continue to revive the child.

It was too late. He blames himself for not being there. It was his fault to let the innocent child die without his protection.

"It is my fault. I was not successful." As the weeping Lord utter in front of the body of the boy which he treats as his own grandchild.

Then the curse of Laura Villegas was sealed without the full truth of incident.

Starting from that day, the Lord never speaks and never went out of the room. He also steps down as the high priest as his son takes on the position.

The curse manifested when the Laura died. As it was believed that soul of the mother made an arrangement to the spirits.

*C*hapter *S*even

*"Trying to trust your heart more than your mind will
sometimes lead to more joyous present."*

Overwhelming

"Can a clueless soul understand the innocent soul?"

Aфтек тне ентіке дау оf explaining the mystery of Amanda and
her family, Ashley still can't believe that all this information is
real. She already knows about all the stories of the family and the curse
including the contribution that she will do to put an end to all of this.
She is just waiting for one more proof before she then commits.

Ashley was able to see the pain on the eye of the woman she is with
right now. She sees that it was never her fault as she is also a victim on
this ancient curse. Even, as much as she wanted to console and give
affection to the woman, she isn't sure how to execute on it. Some parts
of her is saying a hug or a sweet verbal affection will be sufficient but it
was known that she is never good with intimate actions.

Amanda was just sitting in the corner of her room while reading
some books from her own limited edition collection. From time to
time, she was glancing at her. The conversation took them 5 hours and

she was amazed how many times this lady saved her. Not literally her but through Rodrigo.

The poor guy was living next to her apartment unit back in the States and discretely able to set-up some hidden camera's all over her place. It was a great shock to her seeing her videos from some years ago when she is still new to the company and she experience a meltdown as one example.

She felt introverted when the woman shows her some of the clips. If this lady can see and monitor all her activity, it would be appropriate to ask on more question. She is debating whether she should ask the lady verbally.

"Come on Ashley ask her. You need to know." Saying it to her own as she internally fights the shyness.

"Go on! I can hear your mind remember?" The woman put down the book that she can't even read because it was in another language.

"Right. Hmmmm, do you also watch me in the bathroom?" Now she was all red.

She heard some cough on the lady. "I may need to let you know that I have asked for Rodrigo to set-up a camera there not to pick on you but to insure that you are safe everywhere." The woman being defensive.

"That didn't answer my question." Ashley talked to herself internally again.

"You talk a lot within yourself." Amanda look at Ashley in the eye. This time Amanda is as red as an apple. "I must admit I have watched you in your tub a lot of times." Then the woman looks at the other direction.

"I felt really embarrassed. I don't take care of my physique that much." Ashley was more focus on the view that the woman has seen.

This made the other woman smile. She now gets that girl was not mad at her but she was showing her insecurities on her body. "You clearly don't have an idea how wonderful you are. You got these habit of talking to yourself in the tub and look like you are having a different personality." Then Ashley arched her eyebrow. Then she realized her words. "Opps, don't get me wrong. I am not a mental health professional that can diagnose you. But it was really cute of you doing all of those." Then Amanda smiles.

This view was new to Ash. She was able to see the simple smile of the woman can make her night complete. There was this feeling of contentment when see is seeing how the glow on the eyes of Amanda makes the emotion genuinely expressed. She could not resist but tries to check the feature of the woman entirely. You could not blame her! If she commits on marrying this girl, she should at least be satisfied on her appearance. Which she is.

It was already dark outside. She received a call from the progress of the work on the shack from her secretary. It was now all complete. The house that her mom thought they can share is already done. With the new interior design incorporated that is her idea.

From the long conversation the two never left the room and tries to both be comfortable with each other. Same goes with the request of Ashley to both rest to ease her headache and also see her with her cursed nature.

They have dined together in the room knowing that the room

actually contains its own small dining table. The meal was pleasant with the exchange of glances.

"I see no resistance from you. It would be normal to run away from this kind of obligation and demand." Amanda asked.

"I see no point. It would be a great waste of time knowing you still would chaste me down. Am I right?" Smart answer from the younger woman.

"That is true. But you must have read my intentions wrong…" Amanda tries to give another information to the girl. "I am not forcing you to do this. All I am asking is try to give me a chance. Get to know me. If you don't feel any attraction towards me the night before the wedding, you can freely go home."

"I am already attracted to you." Another forward answer of Ashley but still in her head. "I am hoping she didn't catch that. It would be so embarrassing." She tried to look at Amanda. She looks normal. It would mean, she wasn't able to hear the woman.

"Do you know that I never tried to have a relationship before? So, I don't know all of these stuff right?" Ashley tries to open another topic while see is in her bed and had her eyes close.

"What I didn't know is how talkative you are…" Amanda laughed out of nowhere that made Ashley smile. She is comfortable with the woman. Out of all the things she gets to know today, the only thing she understand is, Amanda will never harm her. She was her guardian angel and protector.

Out of the hours that they are inside together there was unexpected knock on the door. It was from Ryker. When she answered on the knock and asked for the person to enter, she saw a huge smile from the man and the concern look stating how he was worried on her. Right then when the man landed it's look on the lady sitting on the table couple of meters away from the bed, his smile dropped.

It was understandably a clear disappointment and disbelief. "Amanda, I didn't expect you here." The man shows a rather disappointment reaction.

"The time has come that I would need to share the entire story to Ashley. It would be easier for us from now on." Amanda look at her brother. She was aware of the growing attraction of the man to Ashley. More reason she should act upon this right this moment.

"I will leave you to it then. Ashley, I mean what I said the other night. If you need anything, I am here to help you." The guy then walks out of the room before the woman was able to answer.

"You clearly have grown affection to my dear brother. I might need to tell you that I am feeling deeply jealous about this." Amanda going back to her reading.

"You clearly can't blame me right? You were nearly out and about. So, serious that I fear that you will bite." Ashley joke on the woman.

"I have business to run. I can't leave it on my people. Also, you seem not wanting my company." Ashley is now curious what does this statement from the woman mean.

"Hey, you can't say that." Ashley just reacted casually.

"It was late. I would recommend for you to sleep for the time being whilst I wait for the time of our shifting and I will wake you up." Amanda offer the woman some time to sleep.

Melanie Sacay Lizardo

The Answer

"When the answer is presented in front of you, how often do you easily accept it?"

It was a night with the bright beautiful moon like what she always watches. Ashley was standing in a labyrinth with such a confusing structure designed with green leafy grass with sharp thorns that she never has encountered in her life. To her confusion of how she was able to get in there, she drew farther more on the center of the garden with a great source of light. It was then, she knows that she was not alone. As she strides and near the source of light the sound of someone was becoming louder and louder.

"Vetus quomodo sanies significatur Tacita deficta." The chant of one woman in front of the fire. Another herb was thrown on the fire as the chant continues, "Die vel sal afskil soos die tyd van verskuiwing aanbreek. Sal nooit aanvaar word sodra my bloed u bloed sal vergewe nie. In die nag waar die maan sal huil ... sal die een eeu na die ander skyn." (The skin will peel off as the time of shifting comes. Will never be accepted once my own blood will forgive your blood. On the night where the moon will cry... one century try after another will shine.)

Then the flame of the fire dance like an angry animal. Flaring in direction where life can be destroyed.

Ashley watched as the moon's color change in appearance on its surface. Sealing the offering of grief one mother had experienced.

Then the next visions were something she is not expecting. It was how woman walking through the fire pit and burn herself with the song she always sings for her child when it was still on her womb.

"I left my baby lying here, lying here, lying here. To go gather blueberries…"

She covered her mouth out of disbelief as the first reaction but after she comes to her senses tries to shout as loud as she can to stop the woman yet it seems that the woman can't hear her. She tried to go to the fire but the flame is too big that even meters away from it burns her skin.

When the woman is already out of her sight, then she notes for what cause the accepted death sacrifice of the woman with pure grief and sorrow can never be justified.

She screams and screams on top her lungs uttering, "Why? Why would you end your life like that?"

Then she felt a sudden shake and voice, "Ashley! Ashley wake up." A familiar voice come out of nowhere.

When she opened her eyes, she saw this worried face of a woman. She closes the gap of their body and embrace the woman with all her might. It was an instant reaction to cope with the view she experiences. It was like it was her own skin is the one being peeled off by the fire.

The woman was shock that she was not expecting the said action from Ashley. "You are crying and screaming. Bad dream?" She said while easing the stiffness from the embrace. She wanted this for so long. She cries for even a single touch from this woman.

"Yes. All the same dream since my childhood. This is much clearer now. I do understand it now." The statement of the crying woman.

Then Amanda tries to pull out from the clinch and tries to resurface a distance so they can be of face but failed to do so. The smaller woman clings to her even more tighter.

"Please stay. Give me a minute of this." A soft voice that she never thought will be from the smaller woman. She then put her arms around the back of the woman to give her more compassion. Then another voice from Ashley, "It was my mom. Whom I gave my last hug. Right before she died." Another revelation of sadness and loneliness of the woman.

"I am honored. Although, my brother was the one who got the second after that." Amanda spit out a despise on the memory of seeing her bother hugging the woman.

"There are a lot of people who will give you hugs without any meaning to it but only few will get the hug that you consent and give." Ashley whispers in low voice as she recovers from the dream she had.

Amanda secretly smiled as they both melted on a hug that they both wish would never end. It made her feel that Ashley is choosing to give more affection to her. At least what she hopes…

While enjoying the arms of each other, it was the time of the shifting.

Amanda felt anxious as she is anticipating for her skin to be loose and fell off. Her heartbeat races as her thought of Ashley being scared after the hug break off will be the end of her happiness of this moment. She closes her eyes.

She sobs inside as a tear fell right in her rotten cheek.

"I may need you to prepare yourself on the next thing you're going to see." Amanda trying to prepare the woman for her exposure.

"Did the shift start?" Ashley inquire as she slowly put a distant on each other.

"I am on my devious looks now." Amanda said.

Then with the enough distance Ashley stare at the hand of the woman. She is confused by what does this curse or if the woman is joking on her.

She is seeing Amanda with her perfect feature. "What do you mean you are cursed if your face is perfect as it is. Look at your skin! It was without mark of any form of hurt." Ashley narrated. As if she is under the impression that Amanda is playing on her.

"What do you mean?"

Good Side

"It was the unexpected that surprise us."

Amanda directly run to the nearby mirror to check on her appearance. But before she was able to confirm her appearance, someone storm in the room. Making the door slammed on the walk.

It was Ryker and Rodrigo.

"Amanda, look at me." Ryker showed himself on his sister while touching his own skin which is no longer rotten. It was a face of happiness and shock.

"Would that mean you are successful on breaking the curse? But how? If the code meant for the blood moon to be around as you vow." Rodrigo being on questions.

Amanda tries to look at herself on the mirror and saw her face as perfectly fine and normal. Then she rushes to Ashley and hugged her tight. The strong woman was able to spin the smaller woman around before facing the other two people on the room.

"This should mean something but I am certain that this is something good." Amanda stated.

"So, no more devious image that I should fear about?" Ashley interrupted.

"You should be glad Ash. You won't like our appearance if you saw us with it." Ryker said it with a sad tone.

Then the Amanda faced Rodrigo, "Rod, please call the others. Make sure they are all of the same state and try to see any unusual things. Make sure to gather them tomorrow afternoon to the chamber to meet Ashley and try to seek help to the augur of the tribe."

"Sure, I will." Rodrigo then excuse himself and got out of the room. It was an awkward situation knowing the three are now left alone.

After the deafening silence, Ashley spoke. "Would it be okay if we can all get rested?" Then she fakes a yawn to get rid of the situation.

"I may need to go to my own business then." Ryker then exited the room.

Then it was her and Amanda whose left on the room. "I will leave you for now then." Amanda was half across the room when a small voice emerges.

"I didn't tell you should leave." Ashley then is standing near her wide window and looking at the dark sky. "At least not you…"

"Is there something you want me to do?" Amanda was deeply glad about the fast progress of their relationship. It was also something that the augur told her about few years back. That it would be easy and fast to grow affection to each other.

The woman then turns around to look at the Woman across the room. "Sleep with me."

Chapter Eight

Innocence

"Say for some, Innocence makes you missed awesome things. Not for some, because they go to treasure memories with valued one."

Penitent

"Blaming yourself is a disease that put you in a fire that east up your entire being."

I T WAS THE FIRST SNOW of the year as the regretful Lord comes out for the first time. As the river completely froze to ice, he tries to walk dreadfully like a lifeless cadaver into the icy covering of the before grassy landscape.

All the talk about the death of the innocent boy was covered by the influence of his family. What was not covered is his feeling of grieve...

From the time that the child was in his custody, it has become his routine to play secretly with the child to the point that the child treats him as its own dad. It was a secret that he hid even to the eye of his own family.

The aid that he thought will give happiness to the mother of the child was replaced by unmeasured sorrow.

As he reached the exact spot where the child drowns, he kneels down and tried to punch the hard sheet of ice. As he repeatedly punches the ice, his blood was never a reason to stop him. He wept like no father was able to do so.

He is crying his heart out as he remembers how the child used to sneak up to his room and cuddles to him.

"Baba, I can't sleep on the chamber there are strange noises which wake me up. Can I sleep with you?" The child snuggles around his arm. The face of the boy that others can't see the beauty was like a face of human perfection on his eyes. He sees things in different manner.

Knowing the child was intelligent to be caught by any chambermaid's, he is quite confident that he can still keep the secret by their own. "Did you make sure to lock your chamber?"

"Even without foretelling..." the response of the child as he looks at the Lord with assurance. "Baba, tell me about my mother again."

This is the common night of the two. As the story of how great the mother of the boy that she saved him from the people that want him away. It was a made up story...

"One night as your mother Laura was wondering around the garden to look at the blood moon, there was a dreadful man who come and attack her. But because her might..." the story goes on which concludes that she needs to leave the poor child in his custody to save his life from the man who want to harm him. This made the innocent child think that he has a great heroic mother.

As he hears the ice shattering from a distance with the fast current of water inches below the ice, he wishes that this can take him. He started chanting and calling on to the spirit of the water.

It was known that he has a deep connection with the nature as he grows up with the whispers of the air. He always confides on the rule of the nature. Now, that he sees himself as a giver of sorrow, it was a battle within himself to oppose the powerless Laura in the notion.

"Laura, as I cuddle and give protection to your son. I am actually hoping you'll see my deep desire. The desire to give you happiness and not tear. To give you the world with smile and not with wounds. Be it known that I am guilty and your curse with be of sealed."

The whisper on the death of the weeping mother was all over the county. It also reaches him that night. Although he knew how scared the entire family was for the harmless curse. He didn't utter a word.

"Today! I am calling out to you the God of nature to give justice to the crying soul of Laura and her child. I should make the curse of the innocent soul be true." The lord hears the thunder in the sky and a lighting struck on a tree near the shack.

He continued, "Let the shape of the wealth of this family be the reminder of how we should stand with humility. Let it be that a woman stands with power in the family in place for every man. As my spirit will guide the pure helping heart of my next century generation." Then the ice breaking can be heard not far from him.

"Let their sleep be without real sleep if guilt revolves around the family." The final thought s and curse of the Lord to the entire clan.

"The curse would need a breaker. So be it when one heart learns to remove the guilt and shape one hopeless life to grandeur. As the sadness of an empty life be of known, once the selfish act of my successor breaks the curse even without knowing."

"Be the heartbeat of both uniting heart a map for both smile and laughter that would be heard for the first time." Then eerie of ice shuttering drops the Lord in the strong water. As the water reclaims his life for the favor it gives to his final words.

This then became the true curse of the family not from the powerless sacrifice of the woman on fire but the grieving guilt of the Lord.

After Some Days

"Letting someone see your true desire means choosing them to join you in it."

Vicky and Rodrigo flies back to the states as the secretary need to come back to the main state to get the paperwork's certifying that the project is now completed. Rodrigo confesses her love attraction to the secretary which shock both Amanda and Ashley. Then by the word of Ashley, Rodrigo was allowed to go with Vicky.

As Ashley remember her secretary's message on her departure, "Are you sure that you would take another month off to stay in here?" with the worry that she will be offer to the nature by these whimsical creatures. She just laughs as a cover up response.

"Don't tell me you believe all those age revelation and stories from Rodrigo?" This time Ashley is hearing the doubt of her friend. "Girl, if you are not my boss and if I don't need to do this, I will drag you back home." Then Vicky, hugged her. "They are a psycho don't do what they want."

"You should not worry Vicky. I am staying for myself. I wish to get this trip on my own terms now." Her safe answer without giving an argument or denial to her friend.

"Hey! You feeling alright?" Ashley was brought back to the present when her was a worried voice from her back emerges. It was Amanda.

"I am good just a little bored in the house." She grows comfortability on the woman starting when she asked her to stay by her side most of the time to get to know her.

"I am hoping you'll give another 2 days for this isolation. After these, the tribe will then let us out. They will see the final sign." The woman is taking about the palm of both successor and the breaker of curse lit up on the blood moon.

"I am not complaining. Maybe we should watch some film in the shack." Ashley accepted the shack papers and also the offer of the tribe to test her after she saw wonders that Amanda can do. She brings her almost everywhere to the point that the meeting of the high priest is overwhelming to her. She then realizes that it was Amanda whom she saw in the shack while she is sleeping.

The woman motions the girl out of the room and ask her to take the woman's hand. Ashley happily accepted. As she was following the Lady of the house down the huge halls. She is secretly checking her out.

She saw a different Amanda after the memorable night of revelation. She was smiling and looking at her lips from time to time and even hug her when the woman realize that she is feeling sleepy. According to her it would be the first sleep that she will have her entire life.

———✥———

They reach the shack and they chose to watch a movie in the open glass living room. Amanda teases her, "I hope you'll get yourself some pillows and cushion on the bedroom to sit it on the huge carpet. I know you sleep in the middle of a movie. I won't carry you again to bed. You are not light."

"You are mean for someone asking for my hand." She jokingly responded and throw a small pillow on the woman. "I am not light huh."

"You need to get your facts straight woman. I asked not asking. I got my answer apparently." The confident woman smirk. This made the younger woman nervous and think deeply.

"You are so cute when you are tense up. Your pupil dilates when you are triggered and your nose move." Amanda added.

"I'll get the pillows for myself. Don't cuddle up with me on the carpet. I'll rather stay on huge space alone. Take the couch." The young woman faces her back to go to the bedroom.

From a distance she heard Amanda's cute response, "We are not even married yet and I am now on the couch zone." This made the young lady smile from her ear.

She is thinking about these sudden shift on her life that doesn't scare her at all. It seems that they are good shift that made her feel something in her heart for the first time. She being around Amanda made her think about how wonderful it was to see the person who cares for you and helped you since you are nothing. But it was more than gratefulness that she felt towards the woman. It might shock random people she told about this but she thinks she is attracted to the woman in all possible ways. Just she doesn't know how to execute those thoughts and emotion.

She then spotted Amanda already resting on the carpet with her own set of cushion on the floor. She arched her brows and look at the woman on the floor.

"Hey! Don't look at me like that." Amanda seems to turn red that Ashley can't understand why. From time to time she is seeing the woman turn red without reason. It is making her worry at times. It looks like she is having an allergic reaction or what.

"I guess I don't have a choice but to sit beside you again." Ashley continue on pushing the patience of the woman. Which she is liking when the serious face of Amanda comes up. It was like she knows she is important to her.

"I always told you this." Amanda sigh and look down to her knees. "You are free to go home anytime. You don't need to do this." She looks at the eye of the young woman. "I wouldn't care about the curse, the tribe and all. As long as you are going to be happy. This is our fight and not yours."

Ashley being guilty on her actions spoke. "I am not staying because I feel obligated or rather guilty to leave you behind." She is stating the truth while staring at Amanda's eyes. "I am staying because I feel that there is this force that is dragging me to believe you. There is unknown mushy feeling that I can't put into words. I am staying for myself." Then Amanda force herself to gently smile although she can see the uncovered emotion of doubt.

The Series

"When can you tell you should stop?"

After some episodes to the series that they are watching, the two woman weren't sure how they become so close to each other. Probably because of the small cute bicker about the characters and the small talk of prediction in between episodes.

"I am right! This really isn't about the ghost. This is about their love story." The emotional account of Ashley as she was wiping her small tears in her cheek.

When she looks at Amanda which is right now had a stream of tears, she become so worried. The pretend strong lady turns to her side to cover and wipe her tears. "This is all nothing." The crying lady explain as she was certain that the smaller woman was able to see her tearing up.

"Are you all right? You never shed a tear for the other tragic movies we had these past few days. You know I am up to details there might be a story you wanted to share?" Ashley being nosy. She has this huge feeling that the woman keeps some personal stories within herself.

"Well, you are wrong there isn't any story. I just find the living character to be someone in so much pain. Waiting for her to visit her in her sleep from the lake is terrible." This is a lie. Amanda has experiences in the past that she needs to leave her past partners to make sure that there would be no child in their family will be born with the curse.

Then Amanda look at the face of the woman. Right then and there the magical moment links their eyes as they both mirror on each other's emotion.

Ashley looks at the charming face of the woman whose surprisingly so sympathetic and compassionate.

"You are sensitive are some point. I like that." Ashley gently close their gap and hug the lady while whispering those lines. The emotion of the woman she is hugging is beyond what Ashley can bare that is why she just jump for a hug rather than seeing the sadness throughout. She knows there are some stories but the woman isn't ready to tell.

"You like seeing me suffer?" Amanda lightly questions while enjoying the clingy actions of the woman that might have no idea what its giving her.

Ashley draw some distance to be of face with the woman.

"I don't mean it that way. Don't over think. Simply, I think seeing you emotional and showing me that you have some feelings too, makes me realize you are but still a normal person." Ashley mention it in sweet tone which made Amanda think about every word. "I wish that I'll know more of what you like and your emotional side."

Amanda couldn't resist no more after a week of full sexual tension and close the gaps of their faces. This is a soft affectionate peck on the lips of the woman. Then she realizes the intrusion that she made and retreat. "I am sorry. I-ii was out of the line." Amanda is now like a tomato.

Ashley shock but wanting the same from the woman tries to ease the tension, "You are sorry for kissing me or you are sorry for not asking?"

Amanda was then able to look at the eyes of the woman. Wondering what will be the proper answer at this situation. After a couple of gulp on her own, there were no words.

"It would hurt if the answer is you being sorry for doing it. Because I want it too." The husky and small voice from the younger woman.

Stunt of the brave confession from the younger woman. Amanda closes her eyes a couple of times to confirm whether she heard it right. Then when she realizes it is on her accord, she made their body perfectly unite for another kiss.

As their soft lips touch with consent this time it was like a volcano eruption in their whole being. She wanted this for so long. Ashley's lip was frozen for some seconds due to inexperience. But the other lips are there to guide her with the rhythm.

As Amanda slowly dances her lips to savior the taste of the other person's lips, she can't stop her heart from beating loudly on her ear. It serves as the music that makes their lips dance like of a waltz on a royal event. She wraps her one hand at the neck of the younger woman who's surprisingly starting to melt on the kiss to secure that the other woman with not go anywhere far.

As she felt the rhythmic responses of affirmation from the lady, this motivated her to deepen the kiss. She softly bites the lower lip of the woman which made her open her mouth a bit. As planned, she slid her tongue inside the mouth of the woman. From the soft passionate kiss, it transitions to an aggressive sensual kiss. Then she felt the hands of the younger woman clung into her neck competing to her dominance. She is hearing the heartbeat of Ashley in her ear which drives her mad.

Then she heard the most beautiful sound that ever existed. The younger woman's moan.

She took this as sign for her to go on. She positions herself on top of the woman which is right now lying down on the floor where they watch the film in. She signals the leg of the woman to give her access to the middle so can comfortably be in between as she levitates herself using her strong knees.

She loses her mind completely with the sensation that the woman is giving her. She cut their kiss and look at the panting woman. She looks in her eye that seems asking for a question that both their body knows.

Ashley was looking at Amanda's eye wondering why the sudden stop. She longs for the tender lips even it was only seconds away. She keeps on looking at she lips and pull the neck of the woman down to her lips again.

This action makes Amanda smile between their kiss. Which hilariously given a growl by the younger woman, "Arrgghh."

They both want more.

Amanda tries to give the woman a time to breathe and move herself on the neck of the panting woman. There she hears more adorable sounds for more. It was wildly uncontrollable release.

Those made her action out of control she can take the woman right now if she will listen to her urges.

Then one soft hand travels from neck to down to her spine and continued to her sensitive stomach which made her shiver. Finally it reaches to cap her bosom.

She wants to go further with the woman however she needs to stop.

She stops and look at the eye of the woman beneath her. Her eye is full of desire and questioning her sudden pause. Then, she smiles. She drops her weight and give the woman a light peck on her lips.

"We need to wait for the right time, Love."

Chapter Nine

"All seasons are not about abundance there comes the winter
where the coldness of heart claims it's warmth from coal."

All things New

"Two overwhelming…"

ASHLEY IS CURRENTLY LOOKING AT the ceiling of the shack that now she owns. She has this feeling of newness. These emotion is making her smile and ponder upon herself. She experienced her first sensual kiss with someone that attracts her. She felt a heat all over her body when Amanda is touching her body. Single touch of her fingers and lips is like an electric flowing into her core.

She takes a moment to look at the face of her lover and remembers how her lips invades her own lips minutes ago.

It was the best moment that they have shared intimately. Although she is sad for the halt of the moment, she trusts Amanda. She also thinks at this point that she isn't ready to go to the next step. She might demand it at the moment that they are in the kiss but Amanda knows that she would regret it if it escalated that fast. She is thankful that the woman understood her more than she understands herself.

Amanda is currently sleeping right now. This is her opportunity to watch the woman that her drawn affection and deep care about.

It was not known to all that Ashley is already seeing her shadow even back in the states. She felt safe and secure around her and now that she is right in front of her she still can't believe her luck in finding the woman that woke her heart of stone. Maybe that is the main reason that even she encounters a lot of suitors back in the day she prefers to feel the comfort of the shadow watching her every night.

Her hand touch the nose of the sleeping woman and trace it down her lips. With these gentle touches she makes it sure that Amanda will not be disturbed. She knows that the woman isn't easily interrupted by her touches because almost every night that they sleep in one bed she repeatedly wonders around the face of the woman.

She giggles from the inside on the sensation that it brings to her own hands. "I still can't say how much I like you. You made me feel these crazy pulse and all the weird signals around my own body." Her talking in her own mind again. She stayed like that for some while as she enjoyed the playing around her lover's face.

Then she decided to prepare some snacks for both of them when Amanda wakes up.

"I can't believe that I am now using the shack's kitchen. I thought this will start from strange journey and end will a formal project completion. Then here comes the wonderful Fernsby- Amanda whom I think will be my lifetime partner."

The woman decides to prepare some pancakes and some vegetable fruit juice mushed together in the juicer. Then a familiar voice emerges from the outside. Then she manages to instantly catch the source of the voice.

"Ashley, would you give me some minutes to talk to you in private?" It was Ryker. The guy that she wonders the whereabouts in these couple of days. He was gone then like a ghost now outside the glass shack asking her for a private talk.

She trusts Ryker and he is her friend. Above all, he is Amanda's twin brother which according to her was one of the high priest in the tribe.

She nods and walk carefully outside the glass shack passing silently the area where her woman was sleeping. She stares at the sleeping figure of the woman and smile before closing the glass door carefully.

Ryker was able to witness how Ashley laid her eyes on his sister. It stunk the heart of the guy.

"Where were you these days?" Ashley as she hugged the man whom been a good hostile in her first week.

"I was out and about these coal business meeting on behalf of Amanda. She sent me so she can stay with you." Ryker while talking was walking through the labyrinth area. He manages it play it cool hiding away his feeling of hurt.

Ashley walk with him so they can find a place to sit. "I am sorry if you need to do that for us." Then she saw a sad face on the man's eye.

"So, by the means of 'Us', I can say you have accepted her proposal." The sad tone from the man.

"I see no harm on it. I fancy her and she gave me attention too." Blunt answer from Ashley.

This was a great surprise for Ryker. Who on earth can easily develop feeling on someone that doesn't even give you enough time to think about the future. Proposal even before courting someone? That doesn't make sense to him.

"Is there any way I can persuade you to run away from this?" Ryker spit a surprising sentence.

"What do you mean Ryker? You should know that it was beyond what we can decide." Ashley trying to make it transactional rather than confessing her feelings to the man. She knows that she likes Amanda but she can't say that to the man whom had confess to her earlier than the revelation.

"Then you are forcing me to act on this with force." The man grabbed the small woman and put a cloth on her mouth which happens to cover her nose as well. With his might the woman got no chance even she fights against his two arms which is wrap around the body of the woman.

Ashley then pass out. Which made it easier for Ryker to carry the woman away from the place.

———〰———

"Amanda, Help me." It was a voice of a panting woman that woke Amanda up from noon sleep. She instantly jumps up and search for Ashley.

"Ashley, where are you?"

She tries to seek her the woman in the bedroom and the kitchen. Then she found a two glass of juices resting in the island of the kitchen with strawberry pancakes.

Ashley should be here somewhere. She then radios all the security on the area. "Lady of the House is missing. I repeat Lady of the House is missing." The code name for her love is Lady of the house. In case of emergency that is set to hide the identity of the person in question from any outsider.

Then she practically whispers in her mind trying to reach the woman in their special connection. She closes her eye and concentrates, "My love, where are you? Tell me where are you and I will rip the head of someone whom will cause you harm." Then she waited for the voice of the woman and hear nothing. This practically made her so mad.

"Alpha, Lady of the house is nowhere to be found. Not in the manor." The voice from the radio echoes through the shack.

Unbelievable, this is surreal. Today was beyond what they deserve. After their first kiss and make out. She won't allow anyone to harm her love.

The Hidden Chamber

"The pain in the heart of the antagonist."

"I am Silverwand. One of the twelve tribe's head priest which is underdog. They see me as never fit in the tribe's counsel. They choose to interfere in my choices. And now! I will choose my own way." The chant of Ryker in his own chamber. It was the ancient alley chamber

where according to the map was the hostile of the child that his kin killed during the water ritual. No one wonder around this area due to the stories of sinister. This makes it his own refuge.

He looks at the face of the woman he once loved. He knows that it was not her but somehow the resemblance was almost incomparably near.

He manages to lie the unconscious body of Ashley to the ancient bed. He walks back and forth and tries to come up with the plan to get Ashley out of the mansion unnoticed. He also has his radio. Where he heard the signal from his sister. This would be a safe spot for him to hide Ashley for now.

He didn't think that his sister can notice that fast that the woman is missing where in fact Ashley didn't make a sound at all.

The entire make out session of the two was painfully witness by Ryker.

"You are mine, Ashley. You are mine." Ryker stated into the air while he nervously pace around the room.

From the first day that Ryker saw Ashley when she was introduced to them as the interior designer. He felt that deep resemblance of the woman to his past partner. He felt like it was another mean joke from her sister to make him uncomfortable.

All through his almost century old life, she always controls him. He always wanted to have a family of his own but always forced not too by his own sister. It was always to the point of almost happiness. Then here comes his sister stopping and doing everything to stop his own happiness.

Almost 19 years ago, he met this wonderful Asian lady in the Island

of Siargao. He lived there for 5 years. He felt free during his stay. Away from his fortune and traditions, he pursues one girl. They lived together on the island.

But soon after his sister traced his location and sends people to get him, the woman he loved was send somewhere he can't locate. The next attempt of his visit on the island it was mention that she relocates somewhere together with her sister.

It was the time that he lost trust in the leadership of his own blood sister. His happiness and love ripped out from his own soul.

He never understood why a woman should lead the tribe in this generation where in fact his dad train him to be the leader. Just because of a ritual that points to his sister then she shines as the most powerful priest on to this generation.

So, when Amanda told the Tribe that Ashley is the person they have been waiting for to cut the curse in the family. He can't believe that her sister will hurt him this way. He will watch them be happy while he will be miserable. That will not happen.

Then he spotted the woman he abducted slowly waking up. He then kneels on the edge of the bed.

Ashley wakes up in a dark stone wall which is extremely cold. Then she remembers Ryker hand covering her mouth with a cloth that is sedated.

"I don't mean to be harsh and take you somewhere without your consent but I need you to wake up on this hell of an experiment." Ryker states to the woman while the woman focuses her eye to the person she thought she knew.

"Where did you bring me Ryker? For heaven's sake, your sister is now worrying. You need to return me." Ashley shaking the man at her side. Although she debates whether the guys are dangerous or what.

"Even in this chamber you are still bringing her name?" Ryker spit out in the floor of the room.

"Ryker, why are you doing this?" Ashley is already hearing the voice of Amanda while the woman is trying to reach her in their special connection. But with the decision of Ashley, she turn down those signal because she needs to know the motif and source of anger of the man she never think would harm her. She deeply believes in the good heart of almost everyone. Even those of the criminal, they are just pressure by elements to do those. She believes that somewhere goodness lies in the heart of everyone.

"I thought you felt the connection on me first? Don't you think that there must have been a mistake on the prophesy? If you are a woman, the successor must be a man like me?" Ryker trying to reason on the belief that he has as he decipher the curse himself.

"Ryker, you are special but I never felt anything else rather than you can be my friend." Ashley utters. "Why do you hate your sister that much?"

"She is a monster Ashley. You got to believe me. She can't make you happy. This lifetime that we have together has been hell." Ryker tries to shout on top of his lungs. "She is heartless. She can't love someone. Believe me she broke tons of Man's heart. How can she love you- a woman?"

This is another shock for Ashley. Does she really know the woman she is sharing a kiss a while ago?

"That was all in the past and I don't care about all of those." Ashley sounding grounded on the trust she has on the woman.

"She doesn't know how to love. She broke my heart. She broke Rodrigo's heart and all other men in this tribe." Ryker lose it and he is screaming in her face with so much anger.

Ashley was starting to feel fear.

After the outburst of Ryker, he left the stone room which Ashley was certain that it was known location near the exact chamber where the meeting was held. The problem is the room is sealed by thick and huge ancient lock that no hair pin can cheat.

The thoughts and doubts that the man tries to lure into her brain bother her however there is still unmeasurable trust that she gives in to the lady of the manor. Amanda needs to express her more however it was already her time and decision to openly shares those. She doesn't want to force the lady with the idea of sharing. Now all she needs to do is reach Amanda.

She needs to warn Amanda. This at least will not worry her woman. She needs to convince her not to act upon this right away. She has a plan in her head.

She need to know why Ryker felt this way to the most wonderful woman she ever met. She smiles when she remembers the night where Amanda keeps on watching her to make sure the nightmares are out of the way. The woman is caring and make sure that she is happy. Even when she nearly fell from the tree she forces to climb on the other day, she stands on guard to ready to catch her. The eye of the woman never left her. It was how tiny smirk of the perfectionist woman made her want to see her more.

"Amanda, it's me. Can you hear me?" Ashley tries to initiates contact with the woman. She stayed silent for quite some while but surprisingly she heard no response.

"No. No. No. This can't be. Why can I hear her but it seems that she can't hear me?"

Ashley tries again, "Amanda? Can you hear me? Please!"

Then she heard the woman talking in her ear. "Ashley, where are you love? I will not give up. I will never lose you again." Hearing the sobbing woman makes Ashley tear up and fall unto her knee.

When things are going great in the woman's life its seems that it will not go easy as usual.

Painful Talk

"It was the person you least expect that can cause more pain than people you expect."

It's been a while that Ashley didn't respond at her in their mental link. She is getting frustrated about this situation. As much as she wanted to rest her thoughts, she can't.

Right at the time she was able to stand and sit herself on the long couch, Ryker walk towards her as if nothing happens.

"Yo- sis, I heard your radio. Did you find Ashley? Is she safe?" The man tapping her shoulder to give her comfort. This pains her more.

"I can't find her." The only words that she manages to out.

"Do you think that she changes her mind and ran away from all of this?" Ryker trying to play on her.

"Why would you think that?" Amanda lock her grudges inside. Even of the denial that she airs out, her mind is panicking of the thought that Ashley refuse to receive her mental communication.

"This is all overwhelming. I mean you put her in a territory that she didn't know." Ryker continues to ploy.

"There are more things you don't know Ryker." Amanda throws shade on her brother. After what they have shared this afternoon she is trusting the desire of the woman for her. She felt how the body and the eyes of the younger lady aches for her. The heart beat and the stares that they exchange. It would pain her more if she lost her to some evil forces.

"You literally thinks she will be useful to you now that I think the curse is actually broken even without the blood moon." Ryker challenge Amanda. "I thought you will abandon her after the curse like any other passed lover you had."

"How can you think like that? I am your sister. You should know me more than anyone else." Amanda trying to express her emotion inside

"Exactly, I know you more than anyone else." Ryker bitterly spoke towards the emotional and angry woman. "Just tell me if you need help, I will now go to my room." The man walks towards the giant stairs to go to his own room.

Ryker has bigger motif to hurt her sister. He was devastated by how she can intrude in his life while she can easily get want she wants. This is beyond the curse that is now gone. He knows that the curse is finally gone. It might be because of what her sister did to the woman that she likes. According to the curse, it need to let the successor have sex with the pure born. It would mean that his sister already got the woman. "I don't care is I will be her second. As long as I can have her back."

She will just hurt Ashley. Ashley will be much happier with him. He will honor the woman even his sister was the first. He doesn't care about that. These are the thoughts that is running inside the man's head.

He is now packing the bags and arranging the chauffer to bring his Jeep outside near the chamber opening. They will leave tonight. He thinks that Ashley's just being confused by this sudden things being presented to her. After some months she will now see how he can be likeable more than his sister.

Chapter Ten

The Sad Love Story

"There are different kinds of love. Love that was not meant for a time. Love that was not meant for the person. Love that was not meant today."

Island

"Who would have thought that as beautiful as the island, it was the same beauty he will find on a woman."

RYKER WAS ABLE TO ESCAPE on his own private guards and manages to board a plane without a trace. With his fake id's and passport that he paid tons to a con, he will now be called Richard. He made sure that it was a country that none of his family can think off. Add to the note an island that is hidden on the eye of tourist.

He bought a cottage in an Island called Siargao. Because of his stack of cash, he can easily get anything he wants. That was not what he wants though, he will live like any ordinary tourist that have decided to stay on the island.

"Mister, do you need anything aside from all that was already purchased on the bungalow?" the person he hired to settle everything he needs on the island.

"I think you got everything covered. Thank you, Juan." He then walks outside the native wooden structured hut. It was a delightful scenery right in front of the white sand beach.

The ocean is calm and the sun is nearly hugging the line on the wide ocean. It radiates the orange reflection on the water that marks the fulfillment on the heart of the young man. He loves and honors his sister but he seems to see no fit on the rules and ideologies of the entire tribe. He sees no fit on the counsel either. He would rather leave it over to his twin sister.

As he continually watches the sunset, there is one remarkable site that captured his eye.

A woman on a conservative one-piece swimwear giggling and running along with a white dog. He was not aware that the area is accessible by any residents. As part of his agreement with the previous owner, this land and area is secluded that even residents don't enter. "Well, definitely not private at all!"

He decided to draw near the lady and act like a bigger person to ask them politely to go away. When he approaches the area nearer then his senses all rush and he can't stop his heart from beating.

People call it a cliché of love at first sight but it seems that this tan woman around 5'2 ft with the rarest amazing beauty with perfect curves get his heart smoothly in seconds their eyes met.

"You must be the new owner?" the sweetest voice from the little girl. As much as he wanted to utter some words he can't. All of the sudden his throat dries up that made it impossible to speak. He is just looking at the beautiful creature in his peripheral.

"Are you okay sir? Is there any problem?" the woman continues on talking. "I hope we are not invading your place? This is my special spot. The old couple who used to live here know me pretty well."

The voice of the little woman amazed him and acts like a lullaby on his ears. All the anguish and intrusion disappear on the sweet smile of the woman.

Ryker was brought to reality when one chambermaid knocked on the door. He requested this individual to carry his luggage that he would need for his plan tonight.

He reached for the knob and open it. In his surprised it was not a maid but rather his sister. "I came to talk about the business on York. I receive feedback that you never reach there?"

The audacity of this woman that seems to care on the Ashley a while ago seems to have moved on to the business mindset. Proving his point that she never really cares on her. "I am sorry sister but it seems that your incapable brother can't take care of the empire like you do."

Amanda was beyond shock on the approach of her brother. But before reacting on the remark she managed to stare at the luggage that was packed, "Where are you going?" There is already a bit of suspicion on the mind of the woman but she turns it down and rather focus on worry for her brother that seems to be running away again.

"The curse is no more. I do think I should get a life out of the county." Ryker seems to keeps it simple.

"I might have no say to that then. But you can't leave at least tonight. I can arrange transportation for you for the night after next." The moon ritual was coming up and it would put any doubt of the tribe on the curse to an end. Let us just say that some of the head priest of the nearby county was not convince that the curse was already broken. It would make sense knowing as they decipher the riddle it needs to have at least a union on the two soul on a blood moon which is just two nights away.

"Alright, just make sure that you won't interrupt my life ever again. We had this agreement that after you became a superhero and all breaking the cruse, we are heading separate ways." Ryker being direct to his sister.

"I do remember that." Amanda then decided to go out of the room and hide her broken emotion. She never has imagined that after all the years of trying to get along with her brother the disgust and anguish of the man is still there.

Memories

"Reason always resurface when actions need justification."

It was already night time and Ryker needs to bring some food down to the chamber to aid Ashley. He was able to get some of the food selection on the cart without anyone being suspicious. How can someone be suspicious if all of the chambermaids are already used to him being done at the chamber with foods at night.

He is hoping that Ashley can get to her senses soon. He then stares at the tropical fruits that are on the cart. It then brought him back to a memory.

"Richard, how many times did I told you not to come by at night in our house? It is a defiant behavior to wonder around at night for ladies at my age and talk to a guy at this hour." Issay utters with fear on her face.

"I could not help it but bring you these meals." He reaches out for a meal box that he personally made for the girl. He after three months of talking and enjoying the company of the woman, he made up his mind and started pursuing the native lady. Unlike what he was used to back in the county, this place has a lot of tradition he needs to go through before getting a lady. Even the courtship is complicated because you need to visit the house of the lady and do housework for her entire family.

"Papang will get extremely mad if he will know that you are here. I might get into trouble." The face of the woman he loves is almost pale in fear. The lady mention it won't be a good idea doing some courtship this early of them knowing the man.

"I told you to let me start courting you in front of your parents that way there would be no hiding and secrets." Ryker is certain that Issay loves him too. They might have shared few kisses just this month and yet the lady fears her dad the most.

"Papang would prefer a Christian guy and you being rich would be another problem." Issay release a thorn in her heart that she carries every time she looks at the man.

Then the sound of Ashley in the nearby chamber made him angry on the disturbance.

"Amanda, I am here. Anyone there? Please help me." The scream of Ashley. He couldn't believe how Amanda manage to wrap her around her fingers. This might not be a way to deal with this.

"Force it is, Ashley. Prepare yourself." Devilish grunt and voice of Ryker echoes in his own head.

He opens the latch on the opening of the chamber that made his captive stop. He then pushes the cart with rusty wheels on the dark stone room. Then he comes eye to eye on the restless woman.

"Ryker, release me and I will not let anyone know about this. I know that you a good person. Please let me leave this hideous place." The crying woman kneel in front of him.

He notices that the knuckles of the woman are bleeding. Then he looks at old door. It was full of scratches. His heart aches on the view but this won't work. He needs to get what he wants.

"Eat this! I will not repeat myself and you won't like seeing what I am capable of doing." He screams using his baritone voice that makes the pleading lady look at him directly.

On the view of Ashley, she feared the transformation of the likeable man to a devious monster by traits. It was accompanied with the sudden shift of appearance from a normal person to a rotting bone with thorns. She witnesses the shapeshifting of the man although according to them this must be healed due to the curse being cut-off.

The woman ran to the opposite side of the room. "Ryker, your face! Your face!" Ashley then hid her face on her palm.

Ryker then rushes to the wooden cabinet with a piece of remaining shattered mirror. Then he saw himself in the withered form. "I got used to this appearance…" while running his not so surprised hand on his corrode face. With the taste of sadness, the man continues his words "and there is one person whom accepted me with this look yet your

Amanda took her away from me." On the instant memory on his tragic past, he walks towards the curled up lady on the corner of the room on her knees. "Now, I will take you away from her." He finally lost every sanity and emotion he has to the young lady.

In an instant, he lifts the defenseless lady and throw her across the room hitting the wall to directly position her on the bed.

Almost

"When life plays a twist and turn, juggling means trading."

It was almost a year that he started to court the entire family of Issay. Mang Pedrito the father of Issay already formed a bound with his and finally allowed the two to come together. Part of the weird culture that this nation possess was the courtship already transition directly to marriage. As one rule of the father of the woman he desires, he must invite his sister to the wedding and let her meet the family.

This might be a problem but he is hoping that her sister can come in secret for him without letting the tribe knows about his near marriage.

"What are you writing about Rick?" Issay asked the woman as she kissed him gently on his cheek. He smiles and felt relax about this.

"As part of our agreement with your papang, I need to send my sister Amanda a letter." He feels positive about this. He loves her sister and he know that she will be happy knowing about the joy he found in this Island.

He looks at the woman who dare to break the odds of accepting him as he is. Issay knew about his shapeshifting and the woman was scared at first but she come around. She mentions that her feelings are stronger than the physical appearance or deformities he has.

Everything is perfect!

That's what he thought. After one week, the nightmare begins.

His sister being the entire tribe and picking him up in their private chopper. People around the area was paid to forget about his brother's visit and even the entire family of the woman he supposes to marry.

It was almost the perfect life that he deserves. Almost happiness.

This gave him the courage to attain vengeance on his own sister. All possible hate he felt was sculptured in his weary heart.

As the air of petrichor run into his nostrils, he rushes to the now panting hurt woman on the cranky billet. He saw the fear on the bawling woman's eye which encourage his desire to avenge his long lost happiness.

"I-ii am bee-egginng you please don't hurt me!" the sniveling woman said as she engulfed her defenseless arm across her body.

Ashley knew that this is the end of her life. The man that she trusted and shared a couple of laughter and trips around the country is a dangerous person. All she did was to pray that a miracle will happen and Amanda will be safe after all of this.

The man climbs on the bed and put his two strong hands on the woman's neck. With the force, the woman gasp for air.

The action made the clear view of the turning red woman, the man laugh. "You have made a wrong choice of person. I am clearly a way better option than my sister." He then releases one of his hand which is prior on the neck to stop the struggling force of the woman. He corners the two arms of the woman and put it on top of her head. "We could be happier if only you chose me." He whispers like a manic person on the ear of the woman.

Ashley managed to recover her breath for the restraint of the man. She cried for more. "Please Ryker. Stop this." Her voice broke as she plead.

The man laugh. "I will show you one way that can make you realize that a woman needs a man. A true man!" He then stands to remove his pants quickly.

The woman took this opportunity to get out of the bed yet the insane man pulled on to her hair. Making an excruciating pain, the hopeless woman was drag back to the bed. For clearly she never had a sexual interaction in the past, she was more fearful when she saw the man's genital on its full stance.

"Kill me! Kill me instead of this. I won't let this happen." The woman found an extreme force to fight back. She kicks the man on his balls. That made the man roll onto the floor.

"Arrrghhh" Ryker drop a tear on his eyes unable to control the pain.

Ashley run to the door and bang it like crazy while shouting, "Somebody help me! Somebody help me! I am here! Please help me." Hysterically kicking the door even, she gains bruises from it.

"You can't escape." Ryker was not able to recover from the pain and pushed the face of the woman to the door. It made her nose bleed as the impact was terribly disturbing. "You can't run away from this. Believe me! You will enjoy and thank me after this."

Then the man tore the shirt of the woman revealing her back and the undergarment. While the woman felt dizzy on the impact on the hit, Ryker planted kisses on the nape of the woman and cup her waist while still pushing the face of the woman by his other hand.

"Learn from this Ashley. Man are stronger than woman. We are made to rule. We are made to decide." The man presses his erection on the bare back of the tiny woman. He must have notice the woman's worn out body and he took this to transfer the woman back to the bed.

Ashley can no longer fight back. She realizes that this is the end. She then utters to her head, "Amanda, I love you. I am sorry." She wishes to the Universe that even these lines made to Amanda in their link she will be happy.

Ryker celebrates when the lady finally gave up. He easily drags the bottom of the lady along with the lingerie that the woman's wearing. "See Ashley. This will be easy for the both of us if you'll behave."

He went up to the lady and forcefully kisses her on the lips. As he receives no response at all from the woman, he traveled down to her neck and then he heard some noises down the hall but he didn't mind.

He continued.

$\mathcal{C}$hapter $\mathcal{E}$leven

Acceptance

"It is more painful when the cause of pain is from someone you dear and know."

Bob

AMANDA IS NOW IN ASHLEY'S room and she still waiting for any feedback from the head of the security. There was no report of someone entering and getting out of the manor without getting viewed on the security cameras. She is aware that this is an inside job. There is someone in the manor that somehow manage to get Ashley. She is certain because Ashley had no clue with the manor's blind spot.

As she tried to relax herself she kneels on the side of the bed and utters some prayers. "I will do anything just please give her back to me. I just wish her safe and I will let her choose whatever she desires. Even it will break my heart."

As a warm liquid drop on to her cheek, there is a smooth finger that wipe it off. This made her open her eyes and look at her side.

"Bob, what are you doing in here? How'd you manage to get in." The woman's both surprised and worried for the child. She became so acquainted with this kid since he visits her on the garden. He is one of the orphan that she granted access to the other building.

"Amanda, there is no time for this. You need to listen to me." Amanda was shock on the serious tone of the child.

"Ashley needs you. She is down in the chamber on the left wing five doors down the hall." The child continued. "You need to be careful. You need to make it on time." The child is dragging her out of the room.

Without asking she ran off the room and shout for her security team. She instantly trusts the boy. Actually she would trust every information about the location of the woman she loved.

She was like a storm that travels fast on the huge halls. She still can't think of how she mange to stride pass the stairs in a minute.

"Alpha." The only voice she heard from the head of the security. This should have been the role of Rodrigo but due to the travel that she granted for her trusted friend. She is left with the next person in charge.

"Quickly get all the keys on the abandoned chamber on the left wing. Specially the fifth door." Then all of the security people gathered and followed her.

Her heart is beating hard as she draws near the room. Then she was stopped by a whimpering voice, "Amanda, I love you. I am sorry." It was the voice of her love. Professing her love towards her but in this situation.

She is certain that the woman is behind that door. She will do everything on her power to get the woman and protect her.

She is now in front of the door. She got the door opened by her security team using a certain key.

It made her perturbed when she recognizes a voice beyond the door. Due to the fact that the door is ancient and full of rust she asked the tell to kick it open.

When the door hit the ground she wonders her eye throughout the area to find the person she came here to see. She quickly found a figure on the old bed.

Her own brother without his bottom on top of the frail woman that is only left with her brassiere and some piece of the remaining cloth of her top.

This despise her!

She ran and pull the head of her brother. And because of her supernatural gift of strength, she made the man flew across the room. Then, she rushes to the man and punch him on his abdomen. He fell down on his knee and finally see the person who made him stop.

"Amanda! My sister! You seem not to know what privacy is." This sentence angered Amanda more. She stared to the man as if she is ready to kill her own blood. "We are having our sweet little moment sis. As you can see, Ashley here is going to get a taste of real man."

"Are you out of your mind? Why Ryker? Why?" Amanda asked for a reason from his brother.

"Amanda. Amanda. Amanda. You owe me something and it is time to pay." Ryker tries to stand and face his twin. His mouth is bleeding. He spits it in front of the lady.

Amanda is aware of what his brother mean. "Melissa. This is about her?"

"Don't you utter her name as if she doesn't mean anything. She is my life and you took her away from me." Ryker exclaimed near the woman. He was about to attack his twin when he saw that every security team is in the chamber. Also, he is aware that the force that the woman have is extraordinary.

"Aries, cover Ashley with your suit." Amanda not forgetting that Ashley is exposed. "Ryker, I told you that your separation to Melissa is something that I have no control over. It was the tribe. Even how many times I tell you this. I didn't receive that letter but Dad did. He summons me to do it for your own good." Amanda explaining.

"The tribe wants the outsider to be dead but–" Amanda was interrupted.

"Melissa Reyes. That is the name. She is not an outsider." Ryker still claims that the woman he loved should have been a part of the family if the marriage is done. This should have not made her an outsider.

"I arrange their escape Ryker. I saved them and send them elsewhere to make sure they still would be safe far away from our family." Amanda interjected.

This information is new to Ryker. He didn't know anything about this but he isn't convinced.

Before anyone of them utters, there was a voice that commented. "Melissa Reyes. Did I hear it right?" Ashley covered by the black suit of the man named Aries screamed.

"Yes. She is my great love until now. Amanda and this tribe took her away from the life with me." Ryker angrily look at her sister.

"Melissa is my aunt!" another revealing comment from the young woman on the bed.

Aunt Lisa

"Puzzle once started will also be completed at the end. Everything will come piece by piece to answer questions."

Ashley is now safe in her room. She is now wearing a robe but still can't move too much because of bruises and cuts she gain from the assault.

She still plays every scenario as Ryker drops to his own knees after hearing what she says about her aunt's identity.

"Where is Issay now?" Ryker asked her.

"She is in States." She answered brief.

Ryker wanted to go to the woman and ask for more but Ashley fear his attempt on closing the distance. Amanda is also quick to cover any possible access.

"I am sorry, Ashley." Ryker seems to come to his senses after he realize that after all his love is actually just his access. He is regretful on hurting the family member of his past lover.

Ryker is crying both from disbelief that he knows now about the location of Issay and regrets on what he had done to Ashley.

Amanda signal to the security team to get Ryker and detain him on one of their private cell. This would be temporary as she needs to decide on this.

"Love, do you want anything to make you feel better?" Ashley look at the woman beside her. Amanda was being gentle as she could because she is aware of her situation. She is still tearing up on what she experiences on the hand Ryker.

"Can you cuddle up with me till morning?" Simple brave attempt of the woman. She doesn't know yet if she can handle someone near but she needs her love near her.

"Are you sure about this? I hugged you a while ago and you-"

The woman was stooped right away by the demanding statement of the woman. "I need you near, Amanda. I need you." Ashley cries.

"Alright. I am here." Amanda quickly got inside the comforter and slowly close their body together.

Ashley is aware that Amanda's doubting about this so she motions herself and snuggle up to her. She cried even more. Her body seems to feel fear from anyone. But she tries to relax herself.

"Ashley, I will never let you out of my sight. I promise. This will never happen to you again." Amanda soothingly rub the back of the woman. She felt like the woman is finally giving in to the hug. "Right love. There you go. This is me. I will not harm you."

"I saw him change skin Amanda. I saw him." Ashley said.

"What do you mean?" Amanda had something in her mind yet still wanted to make sure.

"He's skin and thorn. All of it."

"How could that be possible that shapeshift is in fact the curse is already broken." Amanda now thinks dearly.

Ashley had thing question in her mind that she wanted to ask the woman whom saved her. "How'd you find me if our mind connection is ruined?"

"A little friend of mine on the orphanage nearby. His name is–"

"Bob. Is he?" Ashley asked.

"How'd you know him?" Amanda asked the woman. She might have also forgotten about the child after the rescue. She at least owes him a lot.

"He always visits me at night and also in the shack." Amanda was glad on the revelation of the woman. At least they knew the boy together.

Ashley continued, "I wish to adopt that child actually."

"We can certainly arrange that. We will visit the orphanage right after the blood moon." What was obviously not answered is how the child knew about Ashley's situation.

They will get those once the child will come of face.

There was a silence between the united body under the covers as they feel each other's breathing. Being inside the room with Ashley made Amanda emotional. Although she is trying to hid it away from the now calmed woman hugging her, she shouldn't stop a tear to felt on her cheek.

Who would have thought that she was about to see her lover abused by her brother? It is a disaster and she is confused as to how she will punish the man who was eaten by his broken heartedness. She decided to put that aside and move closer to the body of the wrap around woman. If being much closer to this is possible she should have done.

"Aunt Lisa needs to know about Ryker, don't you think?" The abused yet concern woman stated.

"I leave that choice to you my love." Amanda felt sad that all of this is just because of her dad's failed choice.

"I need to finish this ritual and finally end this so we can all live normal then we will decide." Ashley weakly said.

Melted

"Even metal have their melting point, try it for a heart of stone."

It is overwhelming to Amanda. All the sudden disappearance and the betrayal of her own blood. She is now looking at the woman in her chest as she nuzzles deep in her body.

"Ashley?" Amanda in low voice call for the attention of the lady.

"Hmmmm?" Ashley carries her weak head and face the woman.

"I thought I am going to lose you?" Amanda can no longer hold the emotion inside her and let go of few sobs. "I thought you run away."

Ashley run her hand on the cheek of the woman to wipe it off gently. "How can I do that if I–" Ashley wanted to express her emotions yet fear and shyness covers her. This would be the first in her life that she is to confess.

"I've heard it on our mind link. The moment I am near the chamber." Amanda recalls on the confession of the woman which might have been nicer if without the assault.

"You heard what?" Ashley plays innocent.

Amanda notice the redness on her face and decided to stop the agony of the woman, "Ashley, I love you too."

They both look in the deep warm of their eyes. This closeness and stare obliterates the experience that the younger woman undergone.

"Can I kiss you?"

It was a surprise that it was the younger woman demanded on it. So, Amanda's heart became so happy. Without waiting for any more time, Amanda gently brought her hand on the cheek of the younger woman to pull it into a kiss.

It was gently but full of desire. Amanda made sure her lips are gentle as the injured woman also got few small cuts on her lips.

She is enjoying the warmth of the lips of the woman who currently is leaning in her rested body on the bed. In no time the kiss deepen that opens more demands and urges to her but she is trying to avoid and not rush things for the woman.

Ashley on the other hand was lost in her desire to forget what happen and also to make sure that she it would be Amanda that will be gifted on her first time.

She listened on the voice in her head and heart. She lifts herself not breaking their united lips to position herself on top of the woman. She is now straddling the woman. This made her balance more comfortable to reach for one of the breast of the woman. She gave it a soft squeeze that made the woman take a deep breath and freeze.

This took her by surprise which is expected by the woman in control. She stops and open her eyes to look at the woman with desire. "Please?" Ashley's simple word that echoes in the entire body of Amanda that was like an electric that power her inmost desires buried for ages.

Amanda lifts herself to reunite their lips for a quick second then pulled the robe of Ashley. This made her world stop. It was like the time froze right in this moment. She is seeing the body of the woman she loves. "I-I was not expecting that you are not wearing anything underneath." The polite and contained comment of the arouse woman.

Amanda then made her move to turn them around. She gently put the naked woman in the bed and made her way to the bust of the woman. She engulfs it with her mouth

"Aaahhhhh" this tickles the whole being of the younger inexperience woman. This made the tingling ache in the middle of her thigh more powerful that wish her woman can put immediate attention there.

The moan made Amanda decide to go on further. She needs to be gentle and she needs to prove that it was her pure love that leads to this and not any form of lust.

She runs her tongue over the sensitive tips of Ashley's bust. She stayed there for a while and then move herself even lower. She is watching every reaction on the face of her love as she is travelling all the way down. All she can see in her eyes is agreement and desire for her to continue.

On her way to the womanhood of the person she loves, she drops some slow soft kisses on some areas in her belly and thigh. When she already is in the exact destination, she looks at the woman and asked, "Are you really sure about this?"

Then she saw a fast nod from wanting woman. Then she starts giving her what they both want.

This is certainly the most happiness she had been in her life. Getting the woman, she took care and love in secret for years even she is unsure whether she can return the affection. She gave her freedom of choice. Unlike what the tribe and this curse lead to them believing they don't deserve happiness.

Chapter Twelve

The Night

"Even the oldest code is decoded still some meaning reminds hidden."

Lost

*"When we search for misleading clues, sometimes
the nature calls and gave it all to you."*

I T IS THE DAY THAT the entire tribe waits for. Shockingly, the tribe was able to accept that the ritual is just a celebration for them for the curse is already been broken according to the testimony of the entire manor. No one experience shifting ever again except Ryker which Amanda told them about it.

As their decoder of the ancient works says, it is better to give the ritual to the moon goddess. It would also make sense for somehow it was clear that they need to gather on the occurrence of the blood moon.

"Amanda, what should I wear?" Ashley is currently in front of her closet with only limited option to match the weird occasion.

Amanda Smiles. It seems that Ashley got into her normal estate after their first ever intimate moment. At least she got her glow back and she is jolly around her. With someone else though, the poor young girl still navigates.

"Love, I got something from the seamstress for you. It will arrive after lunch." Amanda continue of getting some paperwork's done.

Amanda is working on a surprise for the woman. She thought of it as a perfect engagement gift.

This is a surprise that Ashley will be glad for sure. She requested for the images and list of children on the orphanage. So they can formally adopt Bob.

The difficulty was Bob happens to have no name legally and it was her whom gave him a temporary name. So she is scrolling through out the page anxiously.

She is weirded out that still after getting through the list twice she was not able to see Bob in it. This might ruin the surprise. She got one resort on this.

They need to go to the orphanage to find Bob.

"Love, would you mind going out down to the orphanage really quick?" Amanda asked the woman.

"What for? Are we going to see Bob?"

"That is the plan. Can you join me?" Amanda stated.

"Of course, is it in this instant?" Ashley can't hide her excitement to see the cute little boy.

They are both in the office of the director of the orphanage. After a lot of praises and welcoming gesture to Amanda because of their contribution to the orphanage, she gets down to the business right away.

"As you may know, I don't have much time. I have an important gathering to host this evening. Why the images and list you have given is not complete?" Amanda bluntly stated.

"My Lady, I don't understand." The director said.

"Your selection is not complete." Amanda said while controlling her anger and frustration. She glances on the wrap around her arm. Ashley is rubbing her arms which surprisingly calms her down.

"I-iii prepare them myself after your call last this morning. They are all complete." The mister seems rather confused.

"Then, where is Bob in here?" Amanda inquires. "You all didn't name him and so I gave him name. He keeps on playing around the manor." The outburst of emotion of the lady.

Ashley was able to observe the stun ever that the woman affects the director. The director's face turns pale. What they didn't expect was the next statement.

"My lady, there's no single child unattended get pass through our security and we gave all the kids names. You might have mistaken. The manor was off-limits after the time you allotted for us."

Amanda look at Ashley. Would it possible that the child is from the nearby community or a child of their chambermaid? She can't be sure about those.

"I remember vividly that he mentions, he lives in the manor and mention the Orphanage."

After some rounds of verification on the children and the description, they never had a record of the child that they wanted to meet. So they have decided to just leave it to the personnel on the manor.

Small Chat

"Tiny moments lead to big memories…"

Ashley is now wearing the all-white dress fiber made from silk glittered by some tiny beads that made it looks like it was the fiber itself that is shining.

It is almost sunset and the moon will peak at exactly twelve. According to the instruction of Amanda, they will be separated in the labyrinth and if the ritual went well a magical light will lead them to each other. So they have limited time to see each other before the last test.

This is also serves as the ritual of soul equivalent to marriage in legal term but more spiritual. It will be the moon goddess will decide if she grants them good companionship.

"What are you thinking?" Amanda startle the young lady who's unconsciously brushing her chair in front of her wooden vanity mirror.

"I don't like to be separated. What if I can't see anything and those myths that you have are not true?" Ashley is worried about this ritual.

"No matter what happen, trust in me. We hold our fate. I can give you whatever makes you happy." Amanda take the hand of her love.

"I trust in you. I still can't wrap all of these rituals in my head." Ashley commence.

"I don't need you to believe in what I believe in. I am just asking you to believe in me." Amanda insist.

Ashley notice the cloak that was around the body of Amanda. It was adorned with rare gems and stones. In its inner layer you can see the curvy figure of the woman. Ashley felt her cheek heat up when she glances at the bulky view of the bust of the woman.

"Ohhhh, I like this on you." Ashley jokingly stroke her hand along the expose skin.

"My love, we can't do anything right now. We need to get this over with and then we can go take care of ourselves." Amanda planted some small kisses on the woman.

Ashley tries to pull her on a deep kiss which she welcomes for a while. Then, she explains. "I will step down as the high priest sooner that I am able to confirm our union. I will move to the states if your life is in there."

Ashley felt astonished on how Amanda is willing to give up everything for her. "We might need to think about it for some time before deciding, babe. You have responsibility that you need to run in the name of your family."

They both look at each other before finally deciding to join the team.

Found

"Let the spirits guide you."

After all the lights was knock off there was a complete darkness. Ashley never knew that there would be no moon. All they told her is a blood moon will shine up the night. Say what, it was all a hoax. There was a cloudy sky that reflects no light.

She was holding an ancient dagger to protect her from someone that invades her personal space without her grant. It was all part of the ritual.

She keeps running and running in this grass labyrinth maze that frustratingly ends her to a dead end. This horrifies her. This seems to be endless with all the fog and spooky grass formation. She might have some undiscovered fear of enclosed area.

She tries to ran on the left. Still ends her on the dead end. She took the other option and lead her to a longer path yet seems to be familiar to her. She is certainly lost.

Not far from the outer layer of the labyrinth, she can hear all the member of the tribe chanting in a language that scare her more.

This is like a nightmare. She decided to get down on her knee tired and look at the sky. "Mom, please guide me."

In an instant she hears a familiar sound, "Are you tired?" It was the boy that they are looking for this morning.

"Bob, why are you here? It is not safe here."

"For you Ashley, it isn't." The boy giggles. "But I will help you to get in the middle. Amanda is already freaking out. You've been here for two hours." The mysterious boy said.

"Why do you know all of this?" Ashley starts to be curious.

"I live here. I am fixing what I did wrong." Bob stated.

"You are a child. You did nothing." Ashley said.

"In your bare eye, I am. But I am not what you think I am. I wanted to cross to the light. I wanted to join father." Bob stated.

"Who's your father?"

"The Lord of this house before all of this happens. My mother judged him wrong that made my dad act on a curse."

"Woooaaahhhh. You are confusing me."

"Just follow me. I am going to make this right for you and Amanda." The small child runs towards some path.

Then the boy started to say something again, "Give me your hand and the dagger."

Ashley comply and handed the boy the dagger. "Then the boy song chants over her hand and cut a small line on her palm."

"What are you doing?" Ashley retrieve her hand and tries to see the wound for herself.

The moment she saw her palm lighting up like a lamp. It is fascinating and surreal that her blood is illuminating the area. She searched for the boy that is now gone.

She lifts it her hand high and tries to run on one opening. In no time, this made her quest easier. The mental communication the couple had has been barred. According to her speculation this is because of the positioning of the moon and spiritual forces.

Then she found Amanda in the center of the labyrinth with her palm lighting up.

She run to her and hugged her. "I love you. Please no crazy things like this." Then she heard the relief chortle from the woman.

The woman kissed her head while the obvious height difference made it easy for the older woman. "I promise this would be the last."

When they look at the sky, the clouds that covers the moon had vanished, it made the entire manor visible because of the blood moon.

"I guess we have finally ended your family whimsical curse without us knowing what it is truly?" Ashley said.

"Bob told me everything. He ended it. It started from him and he ended it." Amanda said.

"The poor child is also involve in your family? Who is he? Where is he?" Ashley states.

"Bob is the boy from the curse. He went to me when I reach the center of the labyrinth. He asked me if I love you. I gladly answer." Amanda said. "He's a water spirit now. He drown by his own fault. He claims that the water spirit present itself to him and invited him to join the river. He likes water and he jumps. My great grandfather is the one whom cursed us all."

"What? So how about the lady of the other family?"

"I don't know but it seems that it had no effect. Now that all of this is over can I ask you one thing." Amanda said.

Ashley look at the woman in the eye and nod.

"Will you marry me?" Amanda pull out a ring from her pocket and stare at the woman.

"But we are already married in this ritual." Ashley arched her brows.

"That doesn't answer my question." Amanda laughed.

"You're funny. Yes. I will marry you again and again given that labyrinth is out of the way." Ashley hugged Amanda.

After all, the curse that made the entire family think that they can control it, is not up to them. It is up to the spirits around them to decide.

The End.

Epilogue

After a year of getting married legally, Ashley decided to run the branch of the company in New Zealand. It would give Amanda still the control over the ministry. Ryker was already forgiven since the family history put a toll on the guy. This was never easy for Amanda to do but surprisingly through Ashley's reasoning she come around.

This leads to Lisa. Lisa and Ryker finally reunites, however due to the difference of their appearance now, Lisa prefer to let their emotion pass. That is what she thinks, Ryker never thought of stopping. As to the whereabouts of Ryker, it leads him back to the States to chase the woman.

"Amanda, what do you think about IVF?" Ashley asked. They are currently in the manor where Ashley decided to stay for good. She never went back to the states due to the plane fright. Ridiculous as it sounds but the existence of this type of fear truly exist.

"So, I am Amanda now love? What did I do wrong?" Amanda clearly didn't catch the next word. Looking worried put down the newspaper and turn to face her wife.

"Love, what do you think about IVF?" Then it hits Amanda. The eyes of the woman show surprise and excitement. The fact that it was something she wanted to talk about for some time but never had a courage.

"Do you want to start a family with me?" Amanda pulls Ashley's hand and look deeply in her eyes.

"It's about time."

About the Author

Melanie Sacay Lizardo commonly known as Melanie Lear in the publishing world, attempts to fulfill a long overdue goal on sharing her work. She is residing in Cebu Philippines at the moment. She is an Applied Linguistics major which gave her the position in her current company.

She had the fascination on poetry (specifically sonnet), short stories and speeches even at her young age which manifest during her choosing of career. She is currently an advocate for gender equality, protection against domestic violence, and fighting against sexual assault.

There is no much to tell about her but one thing, "Her works spill something about her life."

If you wish to get to know her and reach her please reach her at her email address: lizardoms755@gmail.com || insta: @melanielizardo19

Printed in the United States
By Bookmasters